AGATHA RAISIN AND
THE WITCHES' TREE

The night sky is especially foggy as Rory and Molly Harris, the new vicar and his wife, drive home from a dinner party in the Cotswolds. They screech to a sudden halt when they see a body hanging from a lightning-blasted tree at the edge of town. But it's not suicide; Margaret Darby, an elderly spinster of the parish, has been murdered — and the villagers are bewildered as to who would commit such a crime. Agatha Raisin rises to the occasion, delighted to have some excitement back in her life, but she finds the village poses more questions than answers.

Books by M. C. Beaton
Published by Ulverscroft:

AGATHA RAISIN:
AGATHA RAISIN: PUSHING UP DAISIES
AGATHA RAISIN AND THE
DEAD RINGER

HAMISH MACBETH:
DEATH OF A PERFECT WIFE
DEATH OF A GHOST

DAUGHTERS OF MANNERLING:
HOMECOMING

M. C. BEATON

AGATHA RAISIN AND THE WITCHES' TREE

Complete and Unabridged

PUBLISHER SELECTION
Leicester

First published in Great Britain in 2017 by
Constable
An imprint of Little, Brown Book Group
London

First Ulverscroft Edition
published 2018
by arrangement with
Little, Brown Book Group
An Hachette UK Company
London

The moral right of the author has been asserted

A catalogue record for this book is available
from the British Library.

ISBN 978–1–4448–3859–6

Published by
F. A. Thorpe (Publishing)
Anstey, Leicestershire

Set by Words & Graphics Ltd.
Anstey, Leicestershire
Printed and bound in Great Britain by
T. J. International Ltd., Padstow, Cornwall

This book is dedicated to my sister-in-law, Mona Chesney, with love and affection

SPECIAL ~~MESSAGE TO READERS~~ **ERS**

THE ULVERSCROFT FOUNDATION
(r

research, diagnosis and treatment of eye diseases.
Examples of major projects funded by
the Ulverscroft Foundation are:-

- The Children's Eye Unit at Moorfields Eye Hospital, London
- The Ulverscroft Children's Eye Unit at Great Ormond Street Hospital for Sick Children
- Funding research into eye diseases and treatment at the Department of Ophthalmology, University of Leicester
- The Ulverscroft Vision Research Group, Institute of Child Health
- Twin operating theatres at the Western Ophthalmic Hospital, London
- The Chair of Ophthalmology at the Royal Australian College of Ophthalmologists

You can help further the work of the Foundation by making a donation or leaving a legacy.
Every contribution is gratefully received. If you would like to help support the Foundation or require further information, please contact:

THE ULVERSCROFT FOUNDATION
The Green, Bradgate Road, Anstey
Leicester LE7 7FU, England
Tel: (0116) 236 4325

website: www.foundation.ulverscroft.com

M. C. Beaton is the author of both the Agatha Raisin and Hamish Macbeth series, as well as numerous Regency romances. Her Agatha Raisin books are currently being turned into a TV series on Sky 1. She lives in Paris and in a Cotswolds village that is very much like Agatha's beloved Carsely.

Chapter One

The evening was not going well. The late Agatha Christie would have been amazed to learn that she was destined to be the ruin of some genteel dinner parties. After a move to a village in the Cotswolds, otherwise intelligent people can become keen to 'do the village thing', getting ideas of what it should be like from her detective stories.

That was why Sir Edward Chumble and his wife, Tiffany, had invited the vicar of St Edmund in the nearby village of Sumpton Harcourt and his wife to dinner. 'I mean, one is supposed to invite the vicar,' said Tiffany.

The other guests were Tiffany's friend, Jane Oliver, an odd woman with a look of perpetual bad temper, an elderly judge, Lord Thurkettle, and two 'bright young things', Brenda and Bengy Gentry, who were in fact in their forties but chasing perpetual youth.

The vicar, Rory Harris, was not meek and scholarly. He was built like a rugby prop and had a deep, commanding voice. His wife, Molly, was a truly glamorous redhead, and that put Tiffany, who regarded herself as the fairest of them all, in a vicious temper.

The Chumbles had recently moved to the Cotswolds, and Sir Edward was determined to play the role of squire. But no one touched their

1

forelocks at his approach; in fact, the locals seemed to find him a bit of a hoot. He had retired from the Foreign Office after a brief stint as ambassador in some former part of the Soviet Union that no one seemed to have heard of.

As ambassador, he had hoped to hold grand receptions in a palatial mansion, but the embassy was like a modern bungalow and the locals were insolent.

By moving to the Cotswolds, he fantasised about being head of a little fiefdom: gracious tennis parties, strawberries and cream and all that other lovely old England business. But the village, Cuckleton, although pretty enough, showed a marked lack of interest in the newcomers. To even be considered not worth gossiping about was a sad blow.

Although the vicar and his wife were more down to earth, they had still been rather startled by the grimness of their village, Sumpton Harcourt. It was little more than a hamlet, a group of thatched cottages huddled around a pond, dominated by a blasted oak called the witches' tree. It was said that there had once been a coven in the village.

Tiffany recognised the dress Molly was wearing because she had seen it hanging up in a super-market in Evesham, priced at a mere fifteen pounds. 'So clever of you not to waste money on clothes, Molly,' she cooed across the table.

One of the talents necessary to being a good vicar's wife was the capacity to tell blatant lies. 'You mustn't tease me,' said Molly. 'You know this is Armani. I am just too shockingly expensive, amn't I darling?'

'Worth the money,' boomed her husband. 'Prettiest woman in the room.'

Tiffany took another slug of carefully decanted South African hearty red and said, 'So sorry. But darling, it does look like a Primark one I saw in Tesco's.'

'Poor you,' said Molly. 'I wouldn't be seen dead in Tesco's. Of course, Foreign Offices' pensions must be too dire.'

A maid hired for the evening came in with a trolley of coffee. Tiffany had hired her from a card on the Post Office bulletin board. The maid was called Mrs Batterty and she looked to be in her nineties, which, in fact, she was, being ninety-five years old and creaking with arthritis. She was almost bent double. Pink scalp showed through her thinning white hair. Rory leapt to his feet to take coffee cups from her trembling hands.

When she had tottered from the room, Tiffany said, 'I didn't know she was going to be so old, now, did I?'

'That reminds me,' said Molly, jumping to her feet. 'We've left our darling with a sitter we don't know that well. Got to rush. Must excuse us.'

'Didn't know you had a child,' said Tiffany, escorting them to the front door and giving them each a limp hand to shake.

'We don't. It's our cat. Gets in a frightful state if we're away too long.'

'I could kill that bitch,' muttered Tiffany as she stalked back indoors. She confined herself to imagining she was sweetly murdering the characters of the vicar and his wife. 'So terribly sad,' she told the remaining guests. 'No children. Only to be

3

expected. You see, the poor Church of England does attract closet gays, so they up and marry someone who will play along.'

'But you haven't any children, sweetie, have you?' demanded Brenda Gentry. 'Surely Edward isn't gay? Or was he shagging the peasants when you were out in God knows where? Joke! Don't bristle up. I'll have some more of your box wine.'

'That is a fine vintage,' boomed Sir Edward.

'But I went into the kitchen to see if I could help and there was your missus decanting stuff out of a box of South African red into a decanter.'

'She was leaving a drink for the servant,' said Edward desperately. 'Good God! That the time? Sorry folks. Long day. Must ask you to leave.'

After the guests had left and his wife had gone to bed, Sir Edward remained at the table, brooding over the dirty dishes. Although he adored Agatha Christie detective stories, he saw himself more as Dorothy Sayers's Lord Peter Wimsey. He could feel one of his headaches coming on. How ghastly the Cotswolds had turned out to be. Perhaps it was because they had arrived at the dying end of the year. Come summer and surely he would be asked to open fêtes. His eyes half closed as he went off into a dream of croquet on the lawn, cricket in the field, and strawberries and cream with everything.

'What a shit of an evening,' said Molly who was driving. 'I can hardly see in this bloody fog.'

'You should have let me drive,' said Rory.

'You wanted to drink, remember? Oh, why

didn't you get a parish in Oxford or somewhere where there are lights and shops? Sumpton Harcourt is the arsehole of the world.'

Molly hunched over the steering wheel. A breeze started to move the fog which danced in swaying pillars in front of her headlights, somehow making it even more difficult to drive through than the previous thick fog. As she approached the village, through the shifting fog, she saw the lightning-blasted limbs of the witches' tree, as it was called.

'Look, Rory,' said Molly. 'Some idiot's dancing around in this...' She suddenly slammed on the brakes and screamed, 'It's a body!'

Rory got a torch out of the glove compartment, hoping against hope some children had slung a dummy up on the branches. But the torch lit up the dead, contorted features of elderly Miss Margaret Darby, one of the church helpers. The vicar took out his mobile and then remembered that Sumpton Harcourt was one of those Cotswold villages which did not have a mobile phone signal. He went back to the car. 'It's old Margaret Darby. Better phone from the vicarage.'

'You go,' said Molly. 'I'd better climb up and make sure the poor thing is really dead.'

It was at moments like these that Rory realised why he had married her.

He handed her the torch and ran off in the direction of the vicarage. Molly climbed up the branches and shone the torch into the swollen face. Fighting down a feeling of nausea, she stretched out a hand to the woman's neck and felt for a pulse. There wasn't even a flicker.

She retreated to the car. How had they failed

the poor woman? She cleaned the brass in the church and arranged the flowers. She had seemed happy enough. If only she had asked for help.

Molly switched on the engine and turned on the heater. After a mere ten minutes Rory came running back. 'Police and ambulance on their way.'

He climbed in beside her and put an arm around her shoulders. 'Did you have any idea she was suicidal?'

'No,' said Molly. 'We only exchanged platitudes. Things like, "nasty weather" and "isn't it cold?"'

'It's a pity they closed down all the village police stations,' complained Rory. 'Where do they have to come from now? Cheltenham? Mircester? Oh, I hear a siren.'

A police car was the first to arrive. Only five minutes later, the ambulance arrived. A policeman donned a forensic suit, mask, gloves and boots and climbed up to examine the body. He shouted down to the paramedics that the body must be left where it was until a forensics team arrived.

'How awful,' whispered Molly through white lips. 'It seems indecent to leave the poor woman hanging there.'

The companion of the policeman who had climbed up to examine the body came over to their car and took down their names and addresses. 'Before you go any further,' said Rory, 'we've had a shock. You can find us at the vicarage round the corner next to the church if you want statements.'

'Very well, sir.'

The vicarage was much as it had been under the tenancy of the previous vicar. It was dark and gloomy even on a sunny day because it was covered on the outside with ivy. There was no central heating and the floors were stone flagged. 'Let's use my study,' said Rory. 'The fire's laid. I only need to strike a match.'

The study did service as a living room because it had the one fire that did not smoke. It was dominated by a large desk with squat, carved legs ending in griffins' heads. In front of the fire that Rory lit were two horse-hair armchairs, slippery and uncomfortable. They kept meaning to replace them but ever since Rory had taken up his new post a month ago, there never seemed to be any time. He was also expected to preach at four other villages. Even Molly was kept busy with parish visits and the various clubs held in the church hall: Women's Institute, Mothers' Union, Baking Night and Bible readings.

Like the Chumbles, they had been seduced by the thought of idyllic village life. Rory had been vicar of a parish in the East End of London. On a good Sunday, the congregation would amount to around twelve elderly people. On a bad one, it would be far fewer as the church was invaded by drunken youths from the pub next door shouting insults. Tired of the hopelessness of trying to bring the word of God to people who did not want to hear it, tired of the squalor, horrified by a final attack they could not even bring themselves to talk about, they had been delighted at the chance to move to the beautiful Cotswolds.

Also, there was a fairly large congregation on Sundays, with people coming from neighbouring villages, attracted by the novelty of a handsome vicar...

They had seemed to live under constant threat in London and both were surprised to feel an undertone of fear in the village. Of course, the weather hadn't helped. Ever since they arrived, it had either been pouring rain or cold nights with thick fog. Then they were inclined to put it down to the village's Tudor buildings with their thatched roofs, crouched round the village green.

'I am so tired,' said Molly, stifling a yawn. 'And to think I believed that once we were in the Cotswolds all that I would have to do was occasionally twitch the lace curtains. Rory!' She sat up straight. 'Why wouldn't that policeman let the ambulance men cut her down?'

'You mean, was she murdered? No. Just routine. Just how car accidents hold everything up on the motorway these days because of Health and Safety rules that say nothing can be shifted until the transport police arrive and you name it has examined the wreckage.'

'The villagers will have gathered to watch,' said Molly. 'Should I be out there with the tea urn?'

'No. They're probably having the time of their lives. You know, there's something ghoulish about them. That's the door. I'll get it.'

Rory came back with two detectives who introduced themselves as Detective Sergeant Wong and Detective Constable Peterson. Wong looked half Chinese and Peterson was a pretty woman with dark curly hair.

'Would you like some tea or coffee?' offered Molly. 'Or something stronger? Detective Peterson?'

'Oh, do call me Alice. I would love a cup of strong coffee and I am sure Bill here could do with one as well. I'll come and help you.'

'I'll begin with you, sir,' said Bill. 'Where were you this evening?'

'We were at a dinner party at Sir Edward Chumble's in the next village, Cuckleton. We left at about eleven o'clock. Molly was driving. The mist made it difficult to see anything.

'Then Molly and I saw the body in the headlights just as the fog shifted. There is no mobile phone signal here so I went back to the vicarage to call and Molly, my wife, climbed up to make sure the woman was really dead. Why did that policeman stop the ambulance men from bringing her down?'

'We have to wait for forensics when there is any death like this,' said Bill. 'So you left Sir Edward Chumble's home at, say, eleven o'clock. Are you sure of the time?'

'Oh, yes. It was a horrid dinner party and I kept looking at my watch and praying, "Bring on the cheese! Oh, please, bring on the cheese."'

'Who else was there?'

'Lady Edward, her aunt, a Jane Somebody, Lord Thurkettle and Brenda and Bengy Gentry.'

'Were you the first to leave?'

'Yes. I hadn't met any of them before and it will be a cold day in hell before I want to meet any of them again.'

'Why do you think you were invited?'

9

'The Cotswolds seem to be full of incomers all determined to do the village thing: you know, go to church at Easter and Christmas, invite the vicar and his wife, drive a four by four, wear green wellies and talk knowledgeably about crops. Because my last parish was pretty rough, I did indulge in a bit of rural fantasy.'

'Hang on until the spring comes,' said Bill. 'It becomes the prettiest place on earth.'

Molly and Alice entered pushing an old, creaking oak trolley laden with coffee cups, cafetière and biscuits. Once coffee was served, Bill and Molly went over her account. When she had finished, he said, 'I'll save you a trip to police headquarters. I'll send someone tomorrow with your statements and get you to sign them.'

'I believe the one traditional thing you do have in the Cotswolds is a Miss Marple,' said Rory.

'Not that I know of,' said Bill.

'But I read about her. Agatha Raisin! That's it.'

Alice said, 'Mrs Raisin is not elderly, nor does she knit. She is a private detective with offices in Mircester. She is rather attractive.'

A picture of the policeman who had climbed the witches' tree came into Rory's head. He had been young and looked to be highly intelligent. 'What's the name of that policeman who examined the body?' he asked.

'That would be PC Harold Turret.' Bill would have liked to elaborate and say that Turret's nickname was Ferret. He not only worked extremely hard on cases but he also had a nasty habit of finding out everything he could about his fellows' private lives. Bill and Alice were secretly engaged

10

because any liaisons between members of the force were frowned upon. Unfortunately the Ferret showed every sign of being attracted to Alice.

'Are you sure,' pursued Rory, 'that it is suicide? She never seemed depressed or anything like that.'

'We won't really know until the forensic team have put in their report. Good evening. Someone will call tomorrow with your statements.'

When they had left Molly said in a small voice, 'Do you think we made a mistake coming here?'

'No,' said her husband bracingly. 'Wait till spring. People say it's marvellous then.'

'Wouldn't it be awful if poor Miss Darby was murdered?' said Molly as they mounted the stairs.

'It wouldn't somehow,' said Rory, 'I feel guilty about the idea of her being driven to suicide and us now knowing she was in such distress.'

The bedroom was cold. It contained one of those mammoth Victorian wardrobes like the one in *The Chronicles of Narnia* and a four-poster bed, but without the hangings, Molly having torn them down.

'Are we going to bed in our muck?' asked Molly.

'You bet,' said her husband, beginning to tear off his clothes. The bathroom was at the end of a long draughty corridor, and a monument to Victorian plumbing.

Molly sat down at the dressing table and began to remove her make-up with cosmetic wipes. Her face looked odd in the old glass, rather like some other Molly than a reflection.

'Hurry up!' called her husband. 'I'm freezing!'

'That's all I am to you,' said Molly. 'A hot water bottle.'

They had only been married a year but had planned to put off having children.

They decided, as they finally snuggled up together, not to have sex that night; decided by that odd marital telepathy that well-matched couples are lucky enough to have. Molly was just drifting off to sleep when a vivid picture of that body rose up in her mind. She could see it in the headlights, high up on the slippery branches of... 'Rory! Wake up!'

'What! Who!'

'It's Margaret Darby.'

'Oh, do go to sleep.'

'Listen. The odd thing about Miss Darby was that she always wore high heels. Not stilettos but not kitten heels either. She still had them on!'

'So?'

'They didn't have any straps. They were patent leather pumps. She was high up in the slippery branches and the branches were gleaming with wet. She couldn't possibly have climbed up in those shoes.'

'There's a song about that,' mumbled Rory sleepily, 'something like "What? In these shoes?"'

'But Rory...'

'Look, if she's been murdered, the police will find out who did it. That is not our job. Don't interfere.'

And neither the vicar nor his wife would have dreamt for a moment of interfering in police work had it not been for the fact that their state-

12

ments were brought to them the next day by Police Constable Turret. Molly thought he had a clever, interesting face, although critics might have found something rat-like about it. He had small, brown eyes.

After they had signed their statements, he asked, 'Any chance of a cup of coffee, love?'

'If you are talking to me,' said Molly, frost in her voice, 'ask properly.'

'Oh, Gawd!' said Turret, giving what he fancied as a jolly laugh. 'One of them women libbers, hey!'

Molly shrugged, suddenly wanting him to go, but she left the room to fetch coffee.

'Have you anything to ask me or are you waiting to patronise my wife again?' asked Rory.

'Sorry about that,' said Turret, making a mental note to make the vicar's life miserable in some way. 'Now, you and the missus are like the first suspects.'

'Like how?' demanded Rory. 'Twenty minutes before we found the body we were taking our leave of Sir Edward. We've signed our statements to that effect.' He got to his feet to open the door for Molly because he had heard the creaking approach of the old trolley.

'I had it all ready in the hope that nice detective would come back,' said Molly.

Turret leapt to his feet. 'Can I help, gorgeous?'

Rory said evenly, 'We can help ourselves. Molly, why don't you find out if Miss Darby had any relatives?'

'Good idea,' said Molly, thankful of the chance to escape. It wasn't Turret's comments that upset

13

her; it was the way his eyes seemed to crawl over her body, and, yes, there was something frightening about him. She decided to go over to Carsely and call on the vicar's wife there, Sarah Bloxby. Sarah seemed to know about everyone for miles around and might know the dead Margaret's relatives.

As soon as she drove out of Sumpton Harcourt she could feel a weight of anxiety lift from her shoulders. The day was dark and misty and drenched fields stretched from side to side.

To her disappointment, when she was ushered into the vicarage drawing room in Carsely, she found another visitor there: a fashionably dressed woman with a good figure, long legs and small bearlike eyes.

Mrs Bloxby performed the introductions. She served coffee and said, 'It must have been very upsetting for you, finding the body.'

'I wish someone would upset me with a dead body,' grumbled her other visitor. 'I've got nothing but lost cats and divorces on the books.'

'Oh, you're that Agatha Raisin,' exclaimed Molly. 'You know, if we had the money, I would be tempted to employ you.'

'Perhaps Mrs Raisin might be interested in a few facts,' said Mrs Bloxby.

Agatha laughed. 'Mrs Bloxby knows I am always interested in dead bodies.'

'You use second names?' asked Molly.

'A bad habit,' said Agatha, 'developed when we had a genteel Ladies' Society here. It's hard to break.'

Molly leaned her back against the feathered

cushions on the old sofa and told them about the dinner party and how they had found the body. The wood fire crackled on the hearth and from outside came the sweet sound of the tenor bell in the church tower. 'The wind must have got up,' said Mrs Bloxby.

At first Molly talked about the dinner party and then how she had found the body. She went on to describe the two detectives and then the visit from Turret. Suddenly, she found herself crying and hiccuping and gasping out how horrible the vicarage was and how beastly the bloody Cotswolds had turned out to be. A box of tissues was placed on her lap and Mrs Bloxby's quiet voice said, 'Drink this'. Molly dried her eyes and took a gulp. It was sweet and warming. 'What is this?' she asked.

'It's dandelion wine,' said Mrs Bloxby. 'Early in the day for alcohol but it contains a lot of sugar.'

'I don't know what came over me,' said Molly. 'I'm pretty tough. It's the village. It's creepy.'

'That vicarage is rather awful,' said Mrs Bloxby. 'So big and nothing changed since Queen Victoria. I'll drive over and see if I can do something to help.'

'We'll go now,' said Agatha. 'Saturday, and not even a date.'

How old was she? Molly began to worry. This Raisin woman was middle-aged but she carried an aura of sensuality. The trouble with being a vicar's wife was that one often had to deal with women getting crushes on your husband. So far, not one had been anything to worry about, but Agatha Raisin might be another matter.

15

Chapter Two

Agatha Raisin was glad of this unexpected event. She was completely out of dreams and obsessions. When she was obsessing about some man, Agatha could forget about how little she valued herself and wrap herself up in a cosy package of rainbow fantasies. She was also lonely. Her ex-husband, James Lacey, a travel writer, was somewhere abroad and her friend, Sir Charles Fraith, was away somewhere as well, and she missed him. Of course, the steady friendship of Mrs Bloxby was always there, but she was *good*, and Agatha did want to kick up her heels and be bad, preferably in bed with some gorgeous man. Not that she would quite admit that to herself because she regarded herself as a feminist.

Agatha had never before visited Sumpton Harcourt. It was one of those many Cotswold villages hidden in a fold of the wolds, off the tourist route. The day had become darker. They were travelling in Molly's car. Agatha wondered whether Molly was a genuine redhead. She was certainly very glamorous to be a vicar's wife. Molly stopped the car suddenly and said, 'There is the witches' tree.'

It was taped off, the tape fluttering in a strong wind.

Black clouds streamed across the sky above it. Two branches rubbed together giving out an odd creaking sound.

16

Agatha Raisin experienced a frisson of excitement.

Surely that sinister tree was a setting for murder.

The Church of England parish of St Edmund was late Norman. A two-storey extension was added in the thirteenth century and the north aisle was added in the fourteenth century. It had a ring of ten bells and a square Norman tower. Beside it stood the vicarage, dating from the reign of George the Third.

Eighteenth-century Georgian buildings are usually beautiful, but the vicarage was so covered with ivy, it was hard to make out any lines of architecture. A vicar's wife in the late nineteenth century had become so enamoured with all things medieval that she had replaced the plain glass in the windows with mullioned ones that cut out even more of the daylight.

Molly opened the door and led the way into the study. 'Do take a seat,' she said. 'They are uncomfortable but this is the only warm room in the house. In fact the whole place is one shitty igloo.' She glanced at Mrs Bloxby's face and said, 'Sorry about my language.'

'It is one of the perils of being married to a vicar,' said Mrs Bloxby placidly. 'One often wants to shout and swear and get drunk.'

'How understanding of you! Oh, here's my husband, Rory.' Molly made the introductions.

Rory looked at Agatha curiously. 'I thought private detectives were ... well ... rather seedy.'

'As seedy as seed cake,' said Agatha cheerfully.

17

'Do you think Miss Darby committed suicide?'

'Yes, I do,' said Rory. 'I would like it to be murder to ease my conscience, because I keep feeling we should have noticed something.'

'The reason I called on Sarah – I may call you Sarah?'

'Yes. Mrs Raisin and I have become stuck in the old ways.'

'I wondered if Miss Darby had any relatives?'

'Oh, yes. I believe she has a sister, Laura. Twins, I think. It was at the Ancombe sale of work earlier this year. Someone said something about Miss Darby and her sister having a tremendous row in front of the white elephant stall.'

'Do you knows where she lives?' asked Agatha.

'No, but I am sure I can find out,' said Mrs Bloxby.

'Mrs Raisin...' began Rory.

'Agatha, please.'

'Well, Agatha, it's a bit premature to go digging around at that stage.'

'Oh, let her dig, darling,' wailed his wife. 'I want to know what drove her to suicide.'

'We cannot afford a private detective and...'

'No, charge,' said Agatha. 'Just curiosity.'

'Coo-ee! It's only me,' carolled a voice from the hall, outside.

'Oh, dear, it's the vamp of Sumpton Harcourt, Felicity Weir. I'll get rid of her.'

But the study door opened and a tall, thin woman with very large feet and hands stood there. Her hair was brassy blonde and her drooping face was heavily made-up. Her sticklike legs ended in stiletto shoes.

'You naughty, naughty man,' she said. 'Killing off the ladies of the parish.'

Rory took her arm and propelled her back out into the hall. 'You really must excuse us. My poor wife has had a bad shock. No, really, call some other time and ring the bell. What if I should mistake you for a burglar and kill you?'

Felicity tottered off down the short drive. She bumped into PC Turret who was just outside the vicarage gates. Always wanting to play centre stage, Felicity seized his arm and said, 'I am so afraid. The vicar has threatened to kill me!'

'Stay right there!' said Turret. He would drag that uppity vicar in for questioning. A night in the cells would bring him down a peg.

The normally shrewd Turret was to realise he had made a dreadful mistake. That bitch of a woman, Agatha Raisin, conjured up a criminal lawyer. Then he had underestimated what he considered the fusty, hassocky, old Church of England, not realising they would not let one of their own be abused in this way, which the bishop and his canon told Inspector Wilkes in no uncertain terms. Over the Bishop of Mircester's purple shoulder, the inspector could see the press marshalling outside and was sure Agatha had summoned them, as indeed she had.

So Rory was released with full and humble apologies and Turret was given such a dressing down that he could feel all his ambitious dreams slipping away. He was suspended for two weeks.

He hated Rory more than ever and he felt like strangling Agatha. He was just leaving the station when he saw Bill Wong heading for Wilkes's office. Turret thought Bill was too close to Alice. Jealousy prompted him to wait until Bill had gone into the office and then listen at the door.

'It's a bad business,' he heard Wilkes say. 'From the preliminary autopsy, it seems as if she was dead already when that suicide was staged. Yes. It does look now as if someone murdered her and tried to make it look like suicide. The sister's coming in to identify the body. Have a word with her. Ask about enemies. Has she always lived in the village or did she come from somewhere else.'

Turret heard someone coming and moved away quickly. If only he could solve the murder. He would wait in his car outside until the sister left and then see if he could take her for a drink or something.

After he had been waiting ten minutes, a police car arrived. Alice Peterson got out of the back and went round and opened the other back passenger door. A thin middle-aged woman got out. Must be the sister, thought Turrock. She'll be getting the same car back. I'll wait and follow it.

After what seemed an age, Alice came out with the woman and they drove off. Glad that he was driving his own car, Turret kept a few cars behind. Alice pulled into the front of the George Hotel. In the bright entrance lights, he got a good look at the sister as he cruised slowly past and round to the hotel car park. She was wearing an old-fashioned musquash coat and a felt hat. Looked as if she had walked out of an episode of *Foyle's War.*

Turret walked slowly round to the front to see

Alice's car disappearing round the corner. He went up to the reception desk and was about to demand the name of the woman in the fur coat when he looked to the right and saw her in the bar.

When he loomed over where she was sitting, she said with a little gasp, 'I have just talked to the police. What do you want?'

'Just a chat.' Turret sat down facing her and waved to the waiter. 'What'll you have?' he asked.

She ordered a double brandy. Turret said he would have the same. His crafty policeman's eyes studied her sheeplike face and then dropped to her hands. No wedding ring.

Waft of expensive scent. She shrugged off the fur coat to reveal a simple black dress adorned with a large, sparkling diamond brooch. Turret blinked. She could have sold that and bought at least a couple of mink coats.

He introduced himself, commiserated her on her loss, and asked her name. 'I am Laura Darby.'

'And not married?'

'I have no intention of ever getting married again.'

'How many times have you been married?'

'Three.'

The drinks arrived. Women with money had the edge on any of their more beautiful sisters, thought Turret. Fat, ugly little tycoons had dazzling blondes. Rich women could take their pick.

He raised his glass. 'Cheers,' he said. 'To happier times.' He had a sudden inspiration. If Margaret Darby had been equally rich then it followed that someone might have been trying to get money out

21

of her. Or already had! And wouldn't pay back.

'Was your sister comfortably off?' he asked.

'Yes.'

'So was anyone after her money?'

'I don't know. We had quarrelled. She said this brooch had been left to her by Mummy but she left it to me and I told Margaret, you are not getting it.'

'Had she been married?'

'No, but she phoned me up last week and hinted that she was going to be married soon and unless I handed over the brooch, she wouldn't invite me to her wedding.'

The trouble with being a common copper, thought Turret sourly, was that one was always kept out of the loop. But if he could get into Margaret Darby's house, he might find evidence of this man that the detectives and forensics might have missed.

Laura stood up, hitching her coat over her arm. 'I am very tired. Goodnight!'

'Will you be here tomorrow?' asked Turret.

'No, I shall be returning to my home until such time as I can look at poor Margaret's house and its contents.'

'You inherit?'

'Goodnight!'

Turrock stood up as well and grasped her arm. 'Just a few more questions.'

Her pale eyes were suddenly shrewd. They fastened on his collar number. 'As soon as I get to my room, I will telephone headquarters and ask them why you are here and under what authority.'

Turret crumpled. 'It was just a chat,' he said.

'You will hear about this further.' She swept off. Turret cursed under his breath.

Then he thought that he could always say that he had dropped into the George for a drink, had recognised her and had decided to see if she had any useful information. She did not have to answer his questions, did she? And so he rehearsed it all in his mind until he began to relax. That hoity-toity air of hers would put Wilkes's back up.

He was determined to go to Margaret Darby's house. As he was leaving the bar, the waiter stopped him and said, 'Your bill, sir.'

'Not my bill, old son,' said Turret. 'Put it on Miss Laura Darby's room.'

Strangely enough, a lot of policemen are sensitive creatures. Many of them don't know it and bury it under a layer of aggression. But in order to suss out which person is lying or which person might be covering something up, a policeman needs his own radar system.

And so it was that when Turret left his car and walked towards Margaret Darby's thatched cottage he felt an air of menace. Margaret's cottage was called IAMHOME, picked out in poker work on a sign by the gate. Turret cursed under his breath when he saw the red light of a cigarette in the darkness. 'Who's there?' he called.

'Who are you?'

'PC Turret.'

'Oh, it's you, me old ferret.' PC Clapper hove into view.

'Want a break?'

'Do I ever, matey,' said Clapper. 'Tell you

something. This place gives me the creeps.'

'I'll look after things for an hour, if you like.'

'Great!' said Clapper. 'I owe you one.'

Turret waited until Clapper had roared off in his car and made his way up the garden path, dimly lit by a streetlight outside the garden gate. The front door was crisscrossed with police tape. Turret made his way round the back of the thatched cottage. He decided he hated thatched cottages. They were like brooding animals. The kitchen door was taped but the window beside it was not. He took out his knife and sprang the catch, listening nervously for any burglar alarm. He slipped on a pair of latex gloves and climbed into the kitchen, knocking a glass off the draining board as he did so. He cursed and sweated and listened but there was nothing but the sound of the wind.

Taking out a pencil torch, he let the light flicker round the kitchen as he eased himself on to the floor. He went out into a narrow passage which led into a square hall. He switched off his torch because there was enough light from the street-lamp outside, shining through the panes of glass in the front door. He tried a door on the left. It appeared to be full of clutter: photographs in silver frames, china ornaments, all on spindly tables. But in the dark recesses of the room, he could just make out an old-fashioned rolltop desk.

'Now,' he muttered, 'let's see what we can find out.'

He bent over the desk. He suddenly sensed a presence behind him and swung round. A cup of ammonia was thrown in his face. He screamed, thinking it was some sort of corrosive acid. Then something heavy struck him on the forehead and he collapsed to the floor.

PC Clapper drove back up. He saw that Turret's car had gone and heaved a sigh of relief. He neither liked nor trusted Turret. Too many whispers and rumours about how he liked to find out something nasty about someone and then torture them with his knowledge. He burped and winced, wondering if he should have eaten that 'Fiery Bit of Mexico' hamburger at that place down on the motorway.

In front of him, the waters of the pond rippled and shone from the light from the streetlamp. It formed a path of white light across the water to the witches' tree on the other side.

Clapper peered over. There was something up in those branches on the far side showing glimpses of white.

'Kids,' he muttered. 'If they've been messing with a crime scene – if it is a crime scene – I'll wake the whole village.'

He unhitched his torch and switched it on. The tree on the far side of the pond appeared to be straddled by the entrance road but in fact was to the left-hand side. Clapper walked round the huge black bole of the tree to where something hung, revolving in the wind, first right, then left. The torch shone on a policeman's uniform and he gave a cry of fright and dropped his torch. Telling himself not to be a fool and retrieving his torch, Clapper shone it up onto the face of the thing. His hand shook as he realised it was some-

25

one's head covered in white plastic.

He called the emergency services for help. Rory Harris, returning from a late-night call, drove up and shouted out of his car window. 'What's up?'

'I think it's Turret strung up and I can't reach him.'

'I'll go,' said Rory. 'We might be able to save him.' He climbed easily up the thick, bare branches. He felt for a pulse but found none. 'He's dead,' he shouted.

'Leave the body,' yelled Clapper. 'It's a crime scene!'

Molly Harris had felt isolated from the world, locked away in the winter Cotswolds. But now the world had come to her in the shape of the world's press, some even coming from as far away as Japan. A dead policeman in a city would not rouse much interest, but one hung up on something called the witches' tree where a dead body had already been found intrigued journalists.

She had learned to wear her oldest, frumpiest clothes because, on the first day of the press invasion, she had gone down to the village shop wearing a short skirt and high heels and had not been amused when her husband had pointed out to her the next day that she was on the front page of the Sun. Molly welcomed a visit from Agatha Raisin because she was feeling very frightened. Her cleaner, a Mrs Dubble, had said there was a witches' coven in the village, but clammed up when Molly had demanded more information.

'Can I offer you something?' Molly asked Agatha.

'To be honest,' said Agatha, 'I would like a gin and tonic and an ashtray. Now, go ahead and lecture me and then we can talk.'

Molly grinned. She put a large glass ashtray down in front of Agatha, opened a cupboard and took out a bottle of gin and then a can of tonic water from the fridge. 'I haven't any ice,' said Molly.

'You don't need it,' commented Agatha. 'This kitchen is freezing. Doesn't the AGA work?'

'We call it the Sagging Aga. It munches packets of firelighter before it goes properly. It's smouldering for the moment.'

'Have you any sort of alcohol you don't like? I mean,' said Agatha, 'the sort of rubbish one buys on holiday.'

'We've a bottle of Spanish brandy.'

'Let me have it.'

Molly brought down the brandy from a top shelf, Agatha unscrewed the top, lifted the lid of the stove and poured a couple of glassfuls into the smouldering coals. She jumped back as a sheet of flame shot up.

'There you are,' panted Agatha. 'Always works a treat. All these old stoves are raging alcoholics.' She managed to get the lid of the stove back on. It was a dismal kitchen, thought Agatha. It had been painted a sort of sulphur yellow. Cobwebs hung in corners of the ceiling where an old wooden pulley for drying clothes dangled in the shadows.

Agatha surveyed the vicar's wife. She wondered if Molly knew how beautiful she was, but the woman seemed free of vanity. Where was her

27

friend, Sir Charles Fraith? Would he find Molly attractive? He came and went in her life as heartlessly as a cat.

'My cleaning woman says there's a coven of witches in this village,' said Molly.

'Mrs Bloxby told me that. But they've long gone. Photographed in *Picture Post* in the fifties, all of them in the nude with their dangly bits hanging and they were the laughing stock of Gloucestershire. And that was the end of the witches. The tree was called that because it was blasted by lightning and hasn't grown a leaf since then. Why did you marry a vicar?'

'Love,' said Molly. 'That's all it takes.'

'Love,' echoed Agatha sadly. 'Oh, well...' She lit a cigarette and watched the smoke rise up to the dingy ceiling. 'So, I would like to help you, but I've a living to make and I can't see anyone hiring me to look into these murders.'

'I think the Cotswolds should come with a health warning,' said Molly. 'It's not full of bucolic country people, little lambkins and Morris dancers. It's damp, cold and the city lights are so far away. It's all the fault of Agatha Christie.'

'She had murders in towns and cities.'

'Yes, but Miss Marple, for example, has a village mind. Justice is always done. I've a bit of an idea. Drink up. You are about to meet one of the biggest bores in the county.'

Sir Edward Chumble was in a deep sulk when Molly and Agatha called. He had rung various newspaper editors to give his views on the murders and all had shown a definite lack of interest.

He had then visited the latest crime scene to give the police and detectives the benefit of his wisdom and had been told by an Inspector Wilkes to 'run along'.

He had a strong feminine streak and promptly was able to price Agatha's clothes as expensive. His wife was out chairing some committee or other. He reflected that even in a backwater country that everyone but Putin had forgotten, his wife had been able to find a committee to chair. Molly did not match up to his idea of what a vicar's wife should be. She was too bold, too glamorous and did not give him the respect to which he always felt entitled. But this Raisin woman was an unknown quantity.

He had considered inviting her to his dinner party but had looked her up on the internet and had decided such a woman would be too bold and unfeminine. But now as he regarded her, he decided she was pretty attractive even though her eyes were too small.

'Agatha is very busy,' said Molly, after the introductions had been made. 'But I said to her, you must come because Sir Edward is an ex-ambassador and has a very shrewd mind.'

'So you are investigating these murders, Mrs Raisin?'

'Agatha, please,' said that lady, giving what she hoped was a winsome smile, but Agatha did not do winsome and so it looked like a grimace. 'As I am a private detective and that is how I earn my living, I said I would do a few checks to please Molly, but I cannot continue to throw up all my other work.'

'But you are very successful?' pursued Sir Edward.

'Very,' put in Molly quickly.

'Harrumph. I am disappointed in our police force. I thought they might like my help but some chap called Wilkes was most dismissive.'

'Always is,' said Agatha.

He relapsed into silence. A clock ticked busily and the November wind whistled through the thatch. A log shifted in the grate. Agatha surveyed him with displeasure. Pompous fool, she thought. He had thinning grey hair above an open-pored face dominated by a large nose crisscrossed with little red veins. Agatha reached for her handbag.

'How much do you charge?' he asked.

Agatha doubled her rates and then said, 'Of course, I halve them for a friend.'

'Harrumph,' he said again. 'Look here. You do consider me as a friend, don't you?'

Agatha grinned. 'This is so sudden.'

He masked a sudden flash of dislike. He wanted this woman to find out the identity of the murderer and somehow let him have the glory.

'I feel it is my duty to do something for the local community,' he said. 'I would like to employ you to discover who is doing these awful things.'

'I shall send someone over with the papers for you to sign,' said Agatha.

'I am not rich,' he said hurriedly. 'I mean, how long are you going to be at it?'

'I don't know,' said Agatha. 'Look, I'll do my best for six weeks and if I haven't found out by then, I'll give back everything you gave me.'

Sir Edward half-closed his eyes. He could see

himself leaning against that fireplace, facing a roomful of press. *I am here to tell you gentlemen the identity of the murderer.*

'And that's that,' said Agatha to Mrs Bloxby that evening. 'It was Molly's idea. Rory told her how the police had sent the old boy away and how his dignity would be so hurt he might hire me to get even.

'This case fascinates me,' Agatha went on. 'But imagine anyone wanting to solve a case out of wounded vanity.'

You, for one, thought the vicar's wife, remembering Agatha's first case. Instead, she cautioned, 'There has always been a nasty atmosphere about that village. Some parts of the Cotswolds, they still practise witchcraft.'

'Pooh! I think witchcraft is just another name for bitch-craft,' said Agatha. 'I'm off to get some sleep.'

But as Agatha walked down the road to her cottage in Lilac Lane, dead leaves danced and swirled in front of her and she was suddenly aware of a feeling of menace. She quickened her steps and was almost running by the time she reached her front door. There were lights on in her living room. She swivelled round and saw Sir Charles Fraith's car parked outside.

With a gasp of relief she hurtled into her sitting room.

Charles uncurled himself from the sofa. 'You look scared. What's up?'

Agatha shook her head as if to clear it. 'Overdose of imagination. Get me a gin and tonic.'

31

Agatha waited until she had taken a gulp of her drink and then surveyed Charles over the rim of her glass. He was as impeccably barbered and tailored as usual. The only man, thought Agatha, who could walk around a bedroom naked and yet looked tailored in his skin.

She gave a little sigh and began to tell him about the bodies on the witches' tree, ending with, 'A Sir Edward Chumble is hiring me to find out who did it.'

'Why? What's it got to do with him?'

'I think he fancies himself as the local squire. Probably wants me to find out who did it and then pose as Poirot.'

'So why come in here looking as if the hound of hell was snapping at your heels?'

'I went to see Mrs Bloxby and, when I left the vicarage, I got this awful feeling that something was stalking me.'

'"*Like one, that on a lonesome road/Doth walk in fear and dread/Because he knows a frightful fiend/ Doth close behind him tread,*" or something like that,' said Charles.

'I wish people wouldn't quote things at me,' said Agatha crossly. 'They're only showing off.'

'I'll come with you tomorrow,' said Charles. 'Tell me more about it. What's this vicar like?'

'Handsome in a sort of rugger-bugger way,' said Agatha. 'Beautiful wife.'

'You said they'd been to a dinner party. That might be a good alibi. "I couldn't have been out there murdering anyone, Officer, because I was having dinner with Sir Edward."'

'Molly seemed to think Margaret Darby had

been killed somewhere else. Of course, it could turn out to be suicide, but Molly said she was wearing heels and the branches of the tree were slippery and wet, so she surely couldn't have got up there herself.'

'So the dinner party isn't an alibi for anyone?'

'Looks like it. I've got to go to the office first. I'll send Toni over with the contract and I'll ask Patrick to get hold of his police contacts and find out what the autopsy has come up with.'

Charles stood up and yawned. 'I'm off to bed. Coming?'

'You go ahead.'

Agatha followed him slowly, wondering if he would be waiting for her in her bed rather than in the spare room, but her bedroom was empty. That night, she was glad he was in the same house as a cold wind whistled around the cottage and odd things rustled and moved in the thatch.

Charles lay awake reading a spy novel. Suddenly he heard an eerie whisper filling the room. 'Go away. Death is coming. Death!'

Darting noiselessly down the stairs, Charles went into the sitting room and found a packet of firelighters by the fire. He raced upstairs again, put the whole packet in the grate of the bedroom fireplace and set light to it. There was a whoosh as flames shot up the chimney, topped with acrid smoke. He heard someone slithering down the thatch and, forgetting he was stark naked, he rushed outside. There was no one in the garden. He ran round to the front. The gate was swinging open. He saw a dark figure at the end of the street and ran towards it. But when he turned the corner of Lilac Lane the only person in sight was the vicar, Alf Bloxby. He scowled at Charles and snapped, 'Get some clothes on!'

'Did you see anyone?' asked Charles. 'Someone was up on Agatha's roof.'

'No. I did not. For heaven's sake, man, cover yourself up!'

'What with?' asked Charles amiably. 'Lilac leaves?' He strode off, giving the outraged vicar a good view of his bottom illuminated in the street-light.

Chapter Three

Both Agatha and Charles were short-tempered the next day when they drove to Sumpton Harcourt in Agatha's car. They had spent a good part of the night reporting the mysterious haunting to the police. And it was a furious Wilkes who had interviewed them. Because of the worldwide press interest, he had left instructions that he was to be told of the smallest clue, no matter what the time. However, he had not been told that the clue involved his pet hate, Agatha Raisin. His dislike for her rose out of the way she solved cases by bumbling about, often putting herself and everyone else in danger, and then getting to the right conclusion by a flash of intuition. Then she would somehow let the press know that it was she who had broken the case and not the police. Alf Bloxby was also grilled. Wilkes longed to arrest Charles for indecent exposure, but knew the wretched man was a friend of the Chief Constable and so took out his fury on the pair by questioning them over and over again.

The day was dark with great gusts of wind sending ragged clouds tearing across a grey sky. 'That's the tree,' said Agatha.

'Looks creepy enough,' said Charles. 'All those thatched cottages. Amazing it isn't on the tourist route.'

'Doesn't cater to tourists,' said Agatha. 'No gift shop, only a rather dreary pub called ... you'll never guess.'

'Don't want to.'

'It's called The Hanged Man. Look! Over there.'

A much-weathered inn board swung in the wind showing a man mounting the scaffold.

'And who was the hanged man?' asked Charles.

'I don't know.'

'Not much of a detective, are you?'

'There hasn't been *time*, geddit?' snarled Agatha. 'This is the vicarage.'

Charles eased himself out of Agatha's Peugeot. 'Must be like living in the middle of a bush,' he said. 'I bet if all that ivy was stripped off, the whole place would fall down. Bet that ivy has eaten deep into the stone.'

'Are you going to help me with these murders or are you going to stand there wittering all day?' complained Agatha.

'May I remind you, you are not my boss. If you want me, and if you have decided to be civil, you'll find me in the pub.'

Agatha opened her mouth to call an apology to

his retreating back but somehow the words would not come out. She had never felt such a resentment towards Charles before. But now, when she saw him, all she could think about was the time they had shared a bed and yet he went on as if ... as if ... dammit, as if she were a male friend.

But at the moment, he's all you've got, nagged her inner governess. And whose fault is that? If you would only stop looking for romance from unobtainable people.

A tear ran down her face. Charles would now be in the pub, sitting in front of a roaring fire.

'The pub's closed,' said Charles's voice behind her. 'Doesn't open until noon. Ring the bell. I'll get a coffee if I have to make it myself. There's a whopping great raindrop cutting a furrow through your war paint.' He took out a clean handkerchief and dabbed at the tear. He smiled and kissed her on the nose. 'Let's go.'

But the door opened and Molly stood there. 'I heard the voices and peeked through the curtains to see who it was. Come in.'

Agatha made the introductions. 'What sort of a sir are you?' asked Molly. 'Hereditary, or did you or your daddy pay enough to the Prime Minister?'

'Is it global warming?' asked Charles plaintively. 'Everyone's accusatory this morning. I am a baronet.'

'Sorry,' said Molly. 'Come into the kitchen. Thanks to Agatha's Spanish brandy recipe, the stove works. The study is better but Rory is writing his sermon and doesn't want to be disturbed.'

As Molly poured coffee and dished out Garibaldi biscuits, Agatha told her about the mysterious voice coming down the chimney in her spare room.

'Someone has discovered you're investigating and pretty quickly, too!' said Molly. 'Look at this. I'm going to show it to the police but later on. Right now, another interview would make me scream.'

She fished in her pocket and handed over a folded sheet of paper. Agatha fished in her capacious handbag and brought out a pair of latex gloves. 'It's a bit late for that,' said Molly guiltily. 'I should have thought about fingerprints.'

'I don't want mine on it,' said Agatha. 'I've had enough of interviews as well.'

The interview was typed in large black letters:
TELL THE RAISIN WOMAN NOT TO INVESTIGATE OR SHE DIES.

'I wonder how they found out so quickly,' said Agatha.

'Edward Chumble?'

'I don't think so. He wants me to take on the case and let him have the glory. He didn't say so but I am sure that's what is behind it.

'Toni should be over there this morning with the contracts. Maybe he'll change his mind,' said Agatha. 'But just in case, I feel we should get over there and rescue her.'

At that moment, Edward Chumble was posing in front of the fireplace, smiling in an avuncular way at Toni Gilmour, Agatha's attractive blonde detective. He was bragging about how he himself had played detective when he had been British ambassador in Carpet Bagger or somewhere.

Couldn't be Carpet Bagger, thought Toni. Edward had a chuffy sort of vowel-swallowing voice. He sounded like Boris Johnson on speed.

He broke off in mid-pontification at the sound of the doorbell. 'I'll get rid of them,' he said with what he fancied was a roguish smile. Toni heaved a little sigh of relief when he returned with Agatha and Charles.

'We came over because someone is threatening me to stop investigating,' said Agatha. 'Did you tell a lot of people I was taking on the case?'

'No, only the wife. That's her now.'

He winced as a spray of gravel from a car making a vicious speedy turn hit the windows followed by a screech of brakes.

Tiffany erupted into the room. She smelled of Miss Dior and recently drunk gin. Ignoring the company, she said, 'Look, Edward, I can't take much more of this rat hole.' She suddenly swung round, noticing Charles for the first time. 'Who's this?'

'Sir Charles Fraith.'

'Do you live around here?'

'Got a place over in Warwickshire,' said Charles.

'Must invite us, mustn't you? What are the rest of you doing here?'

'Agatha Raisin is going to solve these murders for me. Miss Toni Gilmour there is her assistant.'

'Why bother?' jeered Tiffany. 'I know who did it.'

'Bet you don't!' he raged.

'I need sunshine. Take me to Venice and I'll tell you.'

'No. Miss Gilmour, I have signed the contracts,

38

but I hope to see you again, my dear.'

'Tcha!' snarled Tiffany and shot out of the room again. Screech of brakes, more gravel hitting the windows, great roar of engine, and... 'Sound of witch going off on modern broomstick,' whispered Charles to Agatha.

'I shall call at your office tomorrow for a report on your progress,' said Edward.

Agatha wanted to say it was far too soon, but she guessed Tiffany had probably gone to the pub and she wanted to catch up with her so she said she would look forward to seeing him. Edward saw them out and kissed Toni on the cheek before she could escape.

'How can you bear that horrible old man?' complained Toni when they were outside.

Agatha winced. Although she guessed that Edward was about seventy years old and still a good way off from her own age of fifty-three, she was beginning to dread old age. People said, 'The fifties are the new forties.' Rubbish, thought Agatha. You don't have to deal with an incipient moustache at forty or a waistline that thickens at the very sight of a cream cake.

'He's paying,' said Agatha. 'And this lot interests me and if he wants to pay to play the Great Detective, I don't mind. I don't think Tiffany is the first wife. I cannot see her as Madam Ambassadress. I would guess that the first missus hightailed it out of the marriage when she realised that the future was some backwater of the former Soviet Union. I wonder where he was before the last place.'

'I looked it up,' said Toni. 'Innocence, capital of

39

Ugmu-Zoma.'

'Where the hell's that?'

'Africa. Bang in the middle somewhere.'

'Why on earth should the Foreign Office pay for an embassy there?'

'Oil.'

'Let's track down Tiffany,' said Agatha. 'I've a feeling we'll find her in The Hanged Man.'

Agatha was about to drive off when someone rapped on the car window. Agatha turned red with embarrassment. She had forgotten about Charles. 'Alzheimer's setting in?' asked Charles.

'I was preoccupied,' said Agatha huffily.

'Who is he?' demanded Charles.

'There isn't anybody.'

'Funny that. When you are in the grip of an obsession about someone, Aggie, that's when I become wallpaper to be cast off with the dirty laundry.'

Agatha giggled. 'Idiot! I don't throw wallpaper in the laundry basket.'

But the fact was that Agatha longed to fall in love again. Not with Charles. Before she knew it, he would be announcing his engagement to some bit of rich totty. Love, or obsession in Agatha's case, came like a welcome drug, wrapping her in a warm, protective glow.

Tiffany was already seated in a corner of The Hanged Man when Agatha and Charles arrived, Toni having said she would return to the office. She was talking animatedly to a young couple.

'Trolley dolly,' said Charles.

'Keep your voice down,' said Agatha. 'You never know when the politically correct police will

40

pounce. Do you know that any man in Notting-hamshire who lets out a wolf whistle can be charged with a hate crime? If you mean air stewardess, say so.'

'I think that's politically incorrect as well,' said Charles. 'Shouldn't it be steward person?'

'How do you know?'

'I've had a few,' sang Charles. 'I did it my way.'

'Shut up. Tiffany's waving us over.'

'Sit down,' said Tiffany, 'and settle an argument. What is a baronet doing playing detective? Bengy says it's because you two are an item which I think is ridiculous. Brenda says he's one of the county do-gooder lot, and I say he's short of a bob and is earning his keep in more ways than one.'

'Calm down, Agatha,' said Charles sharply, seeing that an angry Agatha was about to stalk out. 'I shall pour a gin and T down on the flames.'

When Charles went to the bar, Agatha smiled her most charming smile except it looked more like a crocodile seeing easy prey. 'Tell me,' she said sweetly to Tiffany, 'are you an old trolley dolly? Charles says you are. I say, surely not.'

Brenda and Bengy shrieked with laughter and clutched each other.

'I was a cabin attendant on Pan World Airlines.'

'And that is where you met Sir Edward?'

'No. I was staying at the Supreme Hotel in Cairo. Look, you are being damned cheeky. The fact that you are working for my husband does not give you licence to be impertinent.'

Charles put Agatha's drink down in front of her and then began to entertain the company with a

41

fund of lighthearted gossip, while Agatha studied them. Bengy and Brenda. They must be the brother and sister who were at that dinner party on the night Margaret's body was found. They did not look alike. Brenda was of the kind described as 'horsey'. She had a thin, anxious face and large hands and feet. Her brother was slim with heavy, fair hair and wide, blue eyes. Two quite deep lines on either side of his mouth and a wariness about the eyes betrayed the fact he was older than he looked.

You can make everything look young these days, thought Agatha, except the eyes. Tiffany's had one of those wind tunnel face-lifts but her eyes are old. She's watching Charles and pretending to be listening but she looks sad.

Tiffany was remembering when she was at the Supreme Hotel in Cairo and the airline went bust, leaving her stranded. Edward, on leave, had tried to chat her up the evening before and she had snubbed him because she had just snared a paying client, her first foray into the world of prostitution. But Tiffany's introduction to that world had been brutal and nasty. Now Edward looked like a lifeline. When she learned he was an ambassador on leave from some unpronounceable place in the middle of Africa, she set herself out to be as classy as possible, inventing a family mansion that had gone along with the horses and hounds because 'poor Daddy' had lost all on Lloyd's. Edward's previous wife had been small and dumpy. He knew he was due for a new posting. Tiffany with her greyhound figure, her masses of blonde hair and her pouting lips was more the image of a wife he wanted. He dreamed of a capital city, Paris or Rome.

So they got married and Tiffany endured the hell of a backwater in Africa, full of flies and flat-eyed feral children, brutalised since the day they were born.

Then came the news of the posting. It was a crashing blow. 'Where is it?' Tiffany had demanded.

'Another place no one's heard of,' Edward replied.

Tiffany jerked her mind back to the present. Charles was asking, 'Why did you move to the Cotswolds?'

'We heard it was pretty. Edward is an Agatha Christie fan and he thinks village life is like it was in the nineteen thirties with bobbing parlour maids and tea at the vicarage. He doesn't want to know anything about the present day.'

'Maybe something nasty happened to him in Africa,' said Agatha.

'Actually, I think it did. I mean, it was enough to traumatise anyone what with so many people with limbs cut off and fear of rebels. We were just a temporary home for all the oil wheeler-dealers. He went AWOL for two days and what a panic there was. They found him in the jungle. He was feverish and gabbling nonsense and, since then, he's moved back in time. Sometimes he talks about what he did in the war, but he was too young for the Second World War. I suggested a psychiatrist, but he won't hear of it. If I were you, sweetie, I'd run a mile.'

43

Agatha felt a sudden flash of sympathy for Tiffany. She must once have been a pretty girl, the sort of pretty girl who thought looks were enough.

'Is it hard being a private detective?' she realised Bengy was asking. 'I mean, in these days of high-tech forensics and DNA, you don't have any of the advantages of the police.'

'We don't have the paperwork, the top-heavy bureaucracy and if we don't solve cases, we go broke while PC Plod keeps his job no matter what. And talking about PC Plod, what happened to that policeman, Turret? Any ideas? Evidently, he was snooping around Margaret's cottage and someone biffed him, covered his head with tape and strung him up in that tree, all while some other policeman was down on the motorway, stuffing his face with burgers. Now, Lady Edward, you said you knew who the murderer was. Who is it?'

Tiffany was about to reply that she hadn't the faintest idea when the pub door swung open and a clutch of press came in, headed by *Morning Britain* reporter, Jerry Leech. His sharp ears picked up Agatha's question and he sailed forward. 'It's the beautiful Lady Edward,' he said. 'Just the one. Think of our readers, crouched over the usual morning's doom and gloom in the news only to have their hearts lifted by a shot of a glamorous blonde.'

He should bottle his compliments and make a fortune, thought Agatha, as Tiffany seemed to lose years. She tossed back her hair and smiled. 'Just the one.'

'Outside,' urged Jerry. 'Only take a minute.'

'Let's follow her out,' whispered Agatha to Charles. 'She might tell the press if she knows something, but I'm sure she just made it up.'

Tiffany was posed beside the pond, her long leather coat opened and one long leg thrust out.

'If Jerry's thinking about a headline along the lines that she knows the identity of the murderer, then he should stop her grinning like a Cheshire cat.'

The rest of the press had followed Jerry over to the tree. Cameras clicked, television cameras whirred while a delighted and rejuvenated Tiffany twisted and turned like a fashion model.

'I'm not going to say anything until I consult my husband,' said Tiffany. 'Talk to me tomorrow.'

'Wouldn't you say Sir Edward was an old snob?' Charles asked Agatha.

'Oh, yes.'

'So he must have been told by intelligence about Tiffany's real background.'

'I should think Tiffany would know that and got the ring on her finger fast.'

Nonetheless, Sir Edward had enough of his marbles left to learn that his wife planned to unmask the murderer in a day's time. He ranted and raged at her until Tiffany said sulkily that she was going to visit an old friend in London.

As she had not returned to the pub, Agatha and Charles decided to call at the vicarage.

Molly ushered them into the kitchen. 'I'm glad you've called. You see, I don't know much about Margaret Darby to help you. But the old vicar's wife is still alive. She's in a nursing home in Broadway. I mean, all I know about Margaret is

45

that she did the flowers and cleaned the brass.'

'What's the old vicar's wife's name?' asked Agatha.

'Dolly Smellie. I think Dolly's for Dorothy, but it is hard to tell these days. A lot of people get christened using nicknames. At least I was christened Mary. You'll find her in Dunmore Nursing Home. It's not right in Broadway but out on the Cheltenham road.'

'Right, we'll be on our way.'

'Must you go so soon?' pleaded Molly. 'I'm a bit scared.'

'I'll stay,' volunteered Charles happily. 'Off you go, Aggie.'

Agatha looked from Charles's catlike face to Molly's beautiful one. 'Where is Rory?' she asked.

'He's over in Ancombe, calling on a sick old lady.'

Agatha left, feeling diminished. Beauty would always win. She decided to call in at her office first and find out what everyone was doing.

Her small staff were all there and looked up in dismay as Agatha walked through the door. Apart from Toni, her staff consisted of Patrick Mulligan, ex-copper; Phil Marshall, elderly and gentle; Simon Black, young and usually in love; and secretary, Mrs Freedman. They were sitting in the area reserved for visitors and on the coffee table was a large box of sugar-coated doughnuts.

'Why is no one working?' demanded Agatha.

'We all finished our jobs by coincidence at the same time and Mrs Freedman brought in these doughnuts so we decided to enjoy a coffee and

46

have some of them before we got on to the next jobs,' said Toni. 'Have a doughnut.'

Isn't it odd, thought Agatha, that I have reached that age when the very sight of a sugary doughnut makes my waistline suddenly tighten as if in the grip of a giant high blood pressure machine. Oh, the hell with it. She selected a particularly fattening one and sank down on to the sofa with a sigh.

'Where's Charles?' asked Tom.

'Right behind you,' said Charles. 'Move over, Aggie. Those doughnuts look delicious.'

'Why did you abandon Molly?' asked Agatha.

'She had to go out on a call. Just like a doctor.'

Molly had in fact said, 'Now you have tried to make Agatha jealous and it hasn't worked, you can go. I don't like it. You're like a cat playing with a mouse.'

Charles had denied it. I mean, he did not care for Agatha so strongly that he would give up the chance to stay and talk to a beautiful woman. Would he? He gave Agatha a puzzled look.

'What's up?' demanded Agatha. 'Have I a smut on my nose?'

'Nothing,' said Charles. 'If you've finished putting on a kilo, let's go.'

47

Chapter Four

Charles insisted they take his car, an ancient Bentley, although Agatha complained a drive in his car made her feel as if she were going to a funeral.

'And nursing homes make me feel as if I'll soon be at my own funeral,' said Charles as he parked outside the Dunmore Nursing Home. 'I wonder how they thought up that name? Someone sarcastic? Could have done more in life? Or memories of Scotland. I envisage a grim matron. "Now, you be taking your medicine, Charles, or I weel get verra angry."'

'Charles,' said Agatha plaintively, 'are we going in or not? Or are you going to sit here wittering all day?'

They climbed out of the car. A blast of wind whistled through the thick shrubbery bordering the short drive. 'Hear that, Aggie?' said Charles. 'That's the souls of the old folk who were so bad in life that their punishment is to live around this place for ever and ever, amen.'

Agatha marched ahead of him, the spindly heels of her shoes digging holes in the gravel. She had begun to obsess about marriage rather than romance. How dreadful would it be to face the years of decrepitude alone? But what if one's partner or husband was the more decrepit? A low branch of a monkey puzzle, blown by the wind, caught at her sleeve and Agatha let out a yell of fright.

Charles caught her round the waist and kissed her firmly on the mouth. She looked at him in a dazed way. 'Come on,' he urged. 'People to detect.'

The door was opened before they could reach it. 'Amazing,' whispered Charles. 'My matron to the life.'

'I saw yiz canoodling in the drive. I am Mrs Bentley, nurse in charge. Still. It iss grand to see a married couple still in love.'

'We aren't married,' said Agatha. She hurriedly made the introductions and said they wished to speak to Mrs Smellie.

'A "sir",' said Mrs Bentley. 'Och, that explains it. Take a seat. I'll see if Mrs Smellie can see you.'

'Explains what?' asked Agatha when she had hurried off.

'In the pocket of her highly starched uniform is a copy of *The Buck's Revenge* which portrays – I only saw the top of the book – a Regency buck glaring savagely down at a quivering heroine. She no doubts thinks I am going to ravish you under the laurels in the drive.'

'You smell that?' asked Agatha. 'It's old folks' pee, barely disguised by lavender air freshener.'

'All I can smell,' said Charles, 'is a waft of institutional meals.'

Back came Mrs Bentley. 'Mrs Smellie will see you now. Follow me.'

Mrs Smellie was seated with others watching an episode of *Coronation Street* on television.

The volume was high. 'We'll chust be having

49

that rubbish off.' Mrs Bentley switched off the television to howls of dismay from the elderly viewers.

'No, put it on again,' said Agatha. 'Can't we talk to Mrs Smellie somewhere else?'

Mrs Smellie, who had looked like a bundle of shawls topped with grey hair, came to life, throwing back her wrappings and revealing a wrinkled face and clever black eyes.

'Put the fecking telly back on, you miserable gauleiter,' she yelled. 'I'll see them in my room in fifteen minutes.'

Mrs Bentley shrugged and switched on the television and left the room.

'Let's wait outside,' urged Agatha. 'I hope that doesn't happen to me.'

'What doesn't?'

'Turning oneself into a foul-mouthed old character. "I am not a sweet old lady and you can't bully me." That sort of thing. So whatever one really was gets buried under layers of an act.'

Charles felt a lot of that description could be applied to Agatha herself.

They waited until the *Coronation Street* theme tune sounded the end of the programme. 'You know,' said Charles, 'I once had this friend who worked on a newspaper and his job was to look through *Hansard* to find out who was changing their name. He said it was odd that a lot of people called Smellie would change their names to something like John Smellie or Robert Smellie, but they wanted to keep the Smellie bit.'

'It is not odd at all,' said a harsh voice in his ear. 'I am of the Somerset Smellies.'

Charles had a mad desire to say he was from the Warwickshire Stinkers but felt Agatha would not forgive him for antagonising the old bird who was now urging them to 'get on with it'.

Tottering on two sticks, Mrs Smellie led the way into a sort of waiting room. 'You'll have heard about the murder of Margaret Darby,' began Agatha. 'What can you remember about her?'

'Pathetic little flirt. After my husband, she was. Here, I got a photo of him. All the women were mad about him.'

Agatha examined a photograph of a small, low-browed, thick-lipped troll of a man. Love is blind, she thought. I'm suddenly fed up with this detective business. I want to go home, sit by the fire and cuddle the cats. She realised the old woman was speaking again.

'Mind you, it's a wonder Miss Darby didn't get married. I mean, all that money!'

'Where did the money come from?' asked Charles.

'Steel. The parents sold the works a long time back, long before the price of steel dropped.'

'So why do you think she didn't get married?' asked Agatha.

The old eyes were suddenly shrewd. 'She lived in a dream world. Read every trashy romance you can think of. She was engaged to John Hardcotte over in Ancombe. Has the garage. Lusty fellow. Then she breaks off the engagement. Lord! Was he ever mad!'

'Anyone else?' pursued Agatha.

She sniffed the air like a questing hound. 'I'm off! Lunch! Boeuf bourguignon.' And with amazing speed, she creaked to her feet and hurried like a racing land crab out of the room.

'This place must cost a mint,' said Charles.

'They all do,' said Agatha. 'A lot of them cheat the clients, or so I've heard, but this one seems OK if the smell of that food is anything to go by. Should we hang around until after lunch or go and visit this John Hardcotte?'

'We can do both,' said Charles. 'Some pub grub at Ancombe and then see if this chap is still at the garage.'

Agatha felt a sudden rush of affection for him, but quickly suppressed it. Somewhere out there was a simply gorgeous man to wrap her dreams around.

The pub in Ancombe had obviously changed owners. Formerly called The Wheatsheaf, it had changed its name to The Drop Inn. It was a Victorian building, built to attract the railways workers in the days when Ancombe actually boasted a railway station. But the brewery that had taken it over had decided to Tudorise it with fake plastic beams, uncomfortable settles and things like brass bedpans which the new owners fondly believed to be some sort of cooking equipment. They sat down on a couple of uncomfortable settles facing each other, Agatha scowling at a sign which said, YE CUSHIONS, 10p EACH.

'I never thought I'd say this,' said Agatha, 'but we would be better eating at my place, and I refuse to pay for a cushion.'

'My bum's numb,' said Charles. 'I remember there's a café by the church.'

'Let's go.' As they left, a waitress with large

52

bosoms spilling over a laced bodice leered at Charles and said, 'Whither off?'

'Oh, shove your tits back in and get a bra,' snapped Agatha.

'My, my, sweetie,' exclaimed Charles outside. 'That poor girl. You're like some sort of wild animal balked of its prey.'

'Oh, hell. Should I apologise?'

'Don't bother. She probably hears worse around closing time. Look, the café is along there.'

The Dingle Dell café was in the old tradition, run by two elderly ladies. It had lace tablecloths and decorated menus. They ordered macaroni and cheese followed by apple crumble and cream. 'There you are,' said Charles. 'Excellent unpretentious food.'

'Pity they don't have a licence,' said Agatha.

'Craving a gin?'

'No, it's just I usually have some wine with a meal.'

'Oh, yeah! Watch it or you'll end up in the Priory rehab centre.'

'Don't be silly. Let's find out where this John Hardcotte lives.'

The garage was at the far end of the village. Because his old Bentley was a gas guzzler, Charles insisted they walk there. Agatha wished she had worn flat shoes and, as the rain began to fall, decided boots would have been even better.

There was only one man working on the engine of a Volvo. He was middle-aged and grey-haired with a strangely empty face: unwrinkled and expressionless. Even when they introduced themselves and explained the purpose of their visit, he exhibited neither anger nor curiosity. He straightened up and wiped his hands on an oil rag. 'I was engaged to Muss Darby.' His voice had a soft Gloucestershire burr. 'Her did lead me on. Then she up and says she's fallen for someone else. Well, my sainted mother, may she rest in peace, always did say I had a tidy business and the women were only after my money. Yes.'

He fell silent, staring out at the now steadily falling curtain of rain outside the double doors of the garage.

'But Miss Darby was a very rich woman,' said Agatha.

'That's the trouble, see. Them rich folks are tighter than the bark on the tree when it do come to money.'

'I know what you mean,' said Agatha. Flicking a glance at Charles. 'But weren't you angry?'

'I dunno. Bit puzzled like. I mean we wasn't officially engaged. Few folks knew about it. There weren't no presents to send back.'

'Who was the man she said she was in love with?' asked Charles.

'Never did say. And I never did ask. The old vicar, maybe he'd know but he died and his missus went to a nursing home.'

'And that's where we've got to go back to,' said Agatha. 'We'll have to ask her who the latest beau was.'

'If you're sure she'll be awake. Don't old folks sleep after lunch?'

'How should I know?' snapped Agatha, ever

sensitive about her age.

'Calm down, *old girl,* or I'll take myself off. I'm getting bored.'

And that was Charles's fatal weakness, thought Agatha gloomily. He flitted from one thing to entertain him to another ... and from one woman to another. Bad husband material. Hard on those thoughts came Agatha's worry that she was not independent enough. Surely today's women weren't hungry for marriage. But then there was that business about children. Perhaps because of her rotten upbringing and drunken parents, she had never craved children. There had been that disastrous marriage to Jimmy Raisin and then the failed one to James Lacey. Jimmy had been a hopeless alcoholic, but James? James, still hand-some enough to turn heads? But he had kept to his old bachelor ways and had not wanted her to work and had started to criticise her clothes. She heaved a little sigh. Somewhere out there was some man who would get down on one knee and say...

'We're here, Aggie. Say goodbye to your dreams.'

'I wasn't dreaming. I was thinking about the case.'

'Oh, yeah? Come on. Back to God's waiting room. Oh, an ambulance is just leaving. One less, I suppose. Oh, look who's rolling up! Two coppers followed by Bill and Alice. I'm getting a bad feeling.'

Agatha was already out of the car, shouting, 'Bill!'

He swung round, his almond-shaped eyes looking at her suspiciously. 'I must ask you what you're doing here, Agatha.'

'We came back to interview Mrs Smellie again.'

'What about?'

'I'll tell you if you tell me. Why are the police here?'

'Sudden death. And yes, the name is Smellie. So why are you here?'

'She was the old vicar's wife and Margaret Darby was engaged and then broke it off and we wondered if she would know who the new beau was.'

'It's probably a heart attack. She was very old.'

'Then why are you both here and not just a uniformed police officer?'

'A Mrs Bentley who seems to be a matron type is muttering suspiciously. Mrs Smellie has no living relatives. We'll see. Now, get out of my hair, Agatha.'

Agatha and Charles drove to the vicarage to tell Molly the latest news. 'How convenient!' exclaimed the vicar's wife. 'But it seems one too many. I think it'll turn out to be a coincidence. Unless she got hold of some nasty hash.'

'Never tell me she was a pothead,' exclaimed Agatha.

'Arthritis. She was crippled with it and in great pain. Someone introduced her to cannabis and she found it relieved the pain a lot. Of course, contrary to what a lot of people think, unless you are a savvy street person, it's not easy to buy.'

'I can't see the stern Mrs Bentley allowing the smell of cannabis to drift along the corridors,' said Charles.

'No, but she could eat it,' said Molly.

'You mean like teenagers and so on who bake up cakes full of hash?' exclaimed Agatha. 'What an amazing fund of knowledge you have for a vicar's wife.'

'You should have seen our last parish.'

'But she can't start baking up cannabis cakes without the smell being noticed or asking for use of the kitchens,' protested Charles.

'I think she would have had some sort of supplier from around here,' said Molly. 'They're encouraged, surely, to take the air in the garden. She could find a quiet spot and puff away. Now, say somebody knows her habits and gives her some hash-laced cakes. It isn't like smoking. People often go on eating more than they should, waiting for that high, the one you get immediately from smoking, they take too much, the heart starts racing and they die of a heart attack.'

Agatha noticed that Charles was regarding the vicar's wife with a mixture of amusement and admiration. She felt a pang of jealousy. Anxious to take centre stage, Agatha said loudly, 'I'll bet someone such as Mrs Bentley didn't like her suspicions being dismissed by the police. Let's go back and see if Mrs Smellie had any visitors after we left.'

'You go,' said Charles lazily. 'If Molly can give me a coffee, I'll drink it and then be on my way.'

'I thought you were helping me!' shouted Agatha and then turned red with embarrassment.

'Aggie, I am not your employee. You've got an office of detectives. Summon one if you think you need help.'

57

Muttering something that sounded like 'ger-rumph', Agatha left.

'That is one very lonely and vulnerable lady,' said Molly after the door had slammed. 'No, you're not getting coffee and I have parish work to do.'

Agatha felt uneasily ashamed of herself. It had been a clever suggestion of Molly's. Charles caught up with her. 'You forgot. No car. I'll drive you to yours.'

'OK,' said Agatha sulkily.

When he dropped her at her car, he studied her brooding face and said, 'I do have my own life and my own things to do, Agatha.'

'I know that,' mumbled Agatha.

As Agatha climbed into her own car, she noticed smoke rising from James Lacey's chimney. So he was home. Agatha hesitated. But down inside her was an old fear of rejection and a longing for it at the same time. She remembered reading some-where that children of unloving parents grew up mistaking rejection for love.

'Psychobabble,' she muttered, driving off, but deciding to call on her ex-husband later.

There was no police presence outside the nurs-ing home. Agatha rang the bell and waited. Eventually Mrs Bentley answered the door. 'Oh, it's yourself,' she said. 'Come in. I think we should be having a wee word.'

She led the way into a side office. She was wearing a plain blue dress with a soft white collar but she seemed, metaphorically, to crackle with starch.

'It's like this,' she said, 'there's not going to be a police enquiry although there will be an autopsy. They say it's a heart attack and, as she was in her nineties, what's the difficulty in accepting that?'

'I've just learned she smoked cannabis,' said Agatha.

'I knew she smoked in the grounds sometimes, but I didnae know it was hash. She was prescribed a cannabis-based drug called Sativex.'

'You seem to believe there is something suspicious about the death,' said Agatha.

'It was like this. Just after lunch, she had a visitor, an old lady carrying a box of cakes. Mrs Smellie had a sweet tooth, but we don't encourage too many sweet things because they put on weight and it hurts their mobility. She only stayed a few minutes.

'I went in an hour later to give her her medicine and she was lying on the floor. The windows were open and a freezing wind was blowing in. There was no sign of any of those cakes or the box they came in. That's why I called the police. I tell you this, Mrs Raisin, don't ever get old because your relatives can poison you, shove you downstairs, and the hospitals or nursing homes can bugger up your medicines, but it all comes down, according to the law, as natural causes. You're old so it doesn't matter. But there were some crumbs on the table. There was that Chinese-looking detective. He seemed intelligent and sympathetic. I was about to suggest he get the crumbs analysed, but he got a phone call ordering him back to the office.'

'Have you still got them?' asked Agatha.

Mrs Bentley pulled a cellophane packet out of a pocket in her dress.

'I'll give you a receipt for that,' said Agatha. 'I also want you to sign a statement and date it, saying you gave the crumbs to me for analysis. I'll send them to the lab in Birmingham and tell them it's a rush job, although with so much DNA stuff now, they're mostly overloaded.'

'Remember, if you ever need a place here, it's a good idea to book in advance.'

'I hope that's a long, long time away,' said Agatha.

'It'd surprise you. It's like folks put their sons down for Eton the day they're born. We've got a waiting list. Look, if there is something nasty in those crumbs, does that mean there's a serial killer on the loose?'

As she drove off, Agatha found herself hoping that the cake crumbs would prove to be innocent. Another murder would bring the world's press back in full strength and that would mean enormous pressure on the police. They'd be everywhere, blocking off Agatha's own investigations. She drove to Birmingham and dropped off the packet of crumbs at the laboratory, wincing as they charged her extra for a rush job, rush meaning two weeks' time at the earliest.

She stopped off at a large supermarket on the road home intending to buy a microwaveable meal but her eye was caught by a glass case of jam doughnuts. Deciding to buy them for James, she picked out three and put them in a box. Feeling tired, she went into the café and bought a cardboard container of coffee to drink in the car. But the smell of sugar from the doughnut box on the passenger seat was reaching out sticky tentacles to all her senses. One wouldn't hurt. So Agatha had one, and, before she knew it, she had eaten all the doughnuts and her waistline felt tight.

Oh, lost youth! Agatha remembered when, not all that long ago, she could wolf down greasy hamburgers and swallow ice cream sundaes and feel fit, instead of bloated and guilty as she was feeling now. When you entered middle age, guilt set in: guilt about failed marriages, guilt about lost chances, guilt about doughnuts. 'Oh, bugger it all!' yelled Agatha to the rain-smeared windscreen.

When James answered the door, Agatha felt a pang of loss. The marriage hadn't worked and she no longer lusted after him, but he was so handsome, he was still a man to parade with a smirk on one's face of see-what-I've-got.

'Come in and tell me about this local murder,' said James.

'Murders,' said Agatha gloomily.

James's living room was the same as she remembered it to be: book-lined, bright fire and impeccably clean. For the first time, looking at the way the magazines were carefully aligned on the coffee table, she wondered if James suffered a bit from obsessive-compulsive disorder. But then, thought Agatha with a rare burst of self-honesty, housekeeping slobs like herself always regard tidy people as obsessive.

Agatha began to tell him all about the murders and how Sir Edward had hired her.

'That's odd,' said James. 'I mean, the man was an ambassador. Why would someone like that employ a sleuth so that he could show off?'

'I think something nasty happened to him in the African woodshed and he went a bit dotty.'

'But you said he got another posting!'

'Yes, but somewhere in the arsehole of the world!'

'It is all very odd. You'd better take me to see him,' said James.

'All right. But don't put him off! I want to solve this case and no one else is going to pay me.'

'Before we go, let's check up on his background.' James picked up his laptop from a nearby table and switched it on. After some minutes, internet in the Cotswolds villages being rather slow, James said, 'Here we are. Harrow and Winchester. Studied Medieval History at Oxford. Got a first. Weedy-looking fellow. Wait a bit. Joined the Foreign Office but on assignment in Gambia. Worked there as military attaché.'

'That can't be him. Let me see. No, James. Although that photo must have been taken some time ago, that's not Sir Edward.'

'Wait till I scroll down. Ah, here he is.'

Agatha peered at the screen. 'Yes, that's my Edward.'

'Most odd. Educated at Stowe School and Sandhurst Military Academy. Five years in the Household Cavalry. No mention of the Foreign Office but next he appears as a lowly information officer in Gambia.'

'I've an idea,' said Agatha slowly. 'Go back to the other Edward Chumble. I wonder. Look! That Chumble was found wounded and has a wife and two kids. It would not surprise me if the Foreign Office got their Chumbles mixed up. I think the ambassador job was a compensation.

'I think it's a bureaucratic muddle,' continued Agatha excitedly. 'I mean, who would think of two Chumbles from different families and different backgrounds ending up in the same type of job? They hear a Chumble is there and want to make it up to him for the shooting. Something like that.'

'I've a pal at the Foreign Office. I'll ring him and find out.' James, after a long talk on the phone, rang off and explained.

The real truth as it emerged some time later was that there was another Edward Chumble, military attaché in Copenhagen. When oil was discovered in the middle of Africa, that Edward was considered a suitable person to oversee British interests and the appointment was so quickly made that it was only after Sir Edward was jerked from a rather lowly desk job at the Foreign Office that the mistake was discovered. To cover up the mistake, Sir Edward was promised a new appointment while the Foreign Office ploughed through the faraway places where an embassy was about to be closed and hit on Carperijag on the far side of Moldavia.

They ignored reports that Sir Edward had gone slightly bonkers in his previous post after having been lost in the jungle, because who cared about a dump like Carperijag, and lately even Putin

63

had lost interest.

'You're making my head ache. Let's go and see the old boy.'

Agatha had forgotten that a man like James would immediately be the focus of Tiffany Chumble's attentions.

James travelled a lot. His travel guides to different places had climbed up the bestseller lists. So his face was always lightly tanned, emphasising the blue of his eyes.

'Edward will be with us in a minute,' gushed Tiffany, all thrusting silicone bosoms and trout pout. 'Are you related?'

'We were married.'

'R-e-aaally!' Drawling the word out and looking Agatha up and down in astonishment, Tiffany then smiled at James. 'So you're available.'

James studied her for a moment and then said, 'Ever since Agatha divorced me, I can't look at another woman.'

God bless the man, thought Agatha, as Tiffany visibly wilted.

Sir Edward came in and was introduced. 'How is progress?' he said, rubbing his thick hands.

'I think Margaret Darby had a new beau and that person is desperate to stop us finding out who he is.' Agatha reported on the garage owner in Ancombe and the suspicious death of Mrs Smellie.

He sat down and pulled out a notebook. 'I'd better write this down. Old memory isn't what it used to be.'

'You can say that again,' muttered Tiffany.

'It really would be nice if someone asked us to sit down,' said James.

'Oh, poor sweetie. Is diddums legs failing him?' Tiffany had not forgiven James for that put-down, because, I mean, just *look* at Agatha Raisin. Fifty if she was a day.

She found Agatha's bearlike eyes boring into her as if that lady had just read her thoughts and began to gush nervously. 'Oh, please sit down. Can I get you something? Coffee?'

'Black, please. No sugar,' said Agatha.

'White for me and one spoon of sugar,' said James.

'Do come into the kitchen and help me, James, and leave the sleuths alone.'

'Sorry. You see, I'm one of the sleuths,' said James.

Tiffany pouted her way out of the room. She'll probably take the opportunity to have a drink, thought Agatha. I could murder one. I could also murder Edward, pompous idiot.

She said, 'Edward, wasn't it confusing when you were in Africa to have someone of the same name also employed by the Foreign Office and also working in Africa?'

'Don't know what you're talking about,' he mumbled.

James joined in. 'But you must remember. When I was at Sandhurst, there was this chap called James Lacey. I've never forgotten him because I once got punished for one of his bits of insolence. Surely you must remember the other Edward Chumble.'

'Oh, yes, yes. Got it. Him. Yes. Well, weedy

chap. Probably pinched the name. Spook. I mean I'm from the Somerset Chumbles.'

'Yes, but wouldn't he have changed to something else if that were the case?' pursued James.

'Oh, for heaven's sake, man, what does this have to do with these murders? Good work, Agatha. Keep at it. Yes, yes. Nose to the grindstone, hey.'

His wife entered carrying a tray with two mugs of coffee. 'Help yourself,' she said.

'Darling,' said Edward. 'Did you know of anyone romancing Miss Darby?'

'I didn't even *know* Miss Darby. She was probably one of those sticklike creatures who haunt the church with their droopy hems and red noses, and God, I hate this dump!'

Tiffany rushed from the room.

'Poor old girl. Must forgive. Very sensitive, yes.'

Agatha sniffed her coffee cautiously. There was an odd smell coming from it. James did the same thing and they both placed their cups back on the tray.

'I will get back to you, Edward, in a few days' time with a further report,' said Agatha. She wanted all at once to get into the fresh air. She began to wonder whether the Chumbles were mad.

Chapter Five

'What do you think she put in our coffee?' asked Agatha. 'It smelled odd.'

'I think she peed in it,' said James. 'Mine smelled of urine.'

'Oh, James, that's going too far. She wouldn't, would she?'

'She might. Agatha, the things women get up to. Why, last time I was in Barcelona, Maria... Oh, never mind. Boring story.'

'Who's Maria?'

'I said, never mind. Look, about this vicar. I wonder what happened during his stay at that last parish. You said it was in the East End of London. It's not easy for vicars to end up with a cushy number like a Cotswold church. Let's find out where the parish was and go there tomorrow.'

I hope Charles comes looking for me and finds me gone, thought Agatha.

Agatha's heart sank as she saw James warming to Molly's beauty. They told her about Mrs Smellie and Agatha asked Molly if she'd heard anything about Margaret Darby having a beau.

'I've asked around but nobody seems to know.'

'She was engaged to some chap in Ancombe but ditched him.'

'Goodness! Margaret!'

'Tell me,' said James. 'Which church did your

husband have in London?'

'Saint Everild. Down by the old East India dock.'

'Was it difficult to get a transfer?'

'No. Amazingly easy. Look, I would like to talk to you but parish work is never ending.'

They said their goodbyes. 'Do you think she made that up?' asked Agatha.

'I'll look it up.' James took out a smartphone. 'Here we are. Seventh-century lady saint. But Yorkshire! What's a church in the south and in London doing being named after her? Oh, here we are. Ship called *St Everild* caught in a huge storm but by some miracle all the crew and cargo managed to ride it out. Ship's owner, Merchant Josiah Symes, built a church as a way of thanks. Pennyfarthing Lane.'

'Molly said it was a rough area,' said Agatha.

'I didn't think they had rough areas in the East End anymore what with the Chinese and Russians buying up London.'

'What time shall we set out?'

'Just after nine. Miss the rush hour.'

After saying goodbye to James, Agatha drove to her office to tell her staff what she was doing. They usually gathered together at the end of the day. To her dismay, Patrick Mulligan was standing over a large cardboard box of jam doughnuts. Toni of the perfect figure was perched on a desk. She waved a half-eaten doughnut at Agatha and said, 'This is my third. They're from a new bakery in town.'

'I had some earlier,' said Agatha. She told them

of the suspicious death of Mrs Smellie and how she and James were going to London in the morning. Perhaps Toni was the only person who suspected that Agatha was often lonely and insecure. If only she and James would remarry. Charles was too fickle. If some deb with money crossed his horizon, he'd jilt Agatha like a shot.

Simon was angry. Agatha was always taking James or Charles with her on the interesting jobs and he was left with dreary divorces or missing teenagers. Patrick was in his sixties and Phil in his seventies and both were glad just to be employed.

Phil was the agency photographer. 'Phil,' said Agatha, 'it would help if you could sneak some photographs of various people who might be a concern in this murder. I'll type out their names and descriptions for you. Still a lot of press around so you won't be much noticed. You can go with him, Simon. Don't say you're a detective. Chat up some of the local women and find out what you can about Margaret Darby. If we can solve that one murder, we'll find out about the others.'

With her usual intuition, Agatha sensed Simon's anger at being left out and had hurried to bring him in, forgetting that with someone as beautiful as the vicar's wife around Simon, and failing to recall the previous disasters caused by Simon becoming obsessed with attractive women, there might be trouble.

She sat at her computer and typed names and descriptions and then ran off several copies.

'You haven't put in your expenses,' admonished Mrs Freedman.

'Tomorrow. Promise,' said Agatha. She was hungry again but told herself it was nothing but gas. She must make amends for those doughnuts. No dinner tonight.

She and James had decided to travel by train from Moreton-in-Marsh as driving in London consisted of sitting in one traffic jam after another.

James had found the name of the parish. 'It's in Hanthall Green,' he said.

'Never heard of it,' complained Agatha, 'and I know London end to end.'

'It's small area near Lewisham,' said James. 'A mixture of African immigrants and white adults on benefits and white youths either robbing someone or in prison.'

'Can't blame them for wanting to get out.'

'Yes, but right down to the Cotswolds? That is odd.'

'What's this church called?'

'You've forgotten. Saint Everild.'

'Not worth remembering,' said Agatha with all the authority of the ignorant.

They got off at Paddington. James gave way to Agatha's insistence that they take a taxi, although he did try to point out that they would end up sitting in a series of traffic jams. This proved to be the case. The fact that Agatha was paying for the cab did not mollify James, despite the fact that it was Agatha's case and Agatha's expenses. He felt men should be in charge and pay for everything.

The taxi finally drew up in a narrow street where half the buildings had been knocked down. 'They're going to clean up this dump,' remarked the taxi driver. 'Want me to wait, missus? Bad neighbourhood.'

'No, thank you,' said James firmly and before Agatha could open her mouth.

The church stood between the demolished houses on one side and boarded-up tenements on the other. No modern cleaning had touched its soot-stained walls. It looked as if it had grown out of the ground, rather than being built by man. It had a square tower from which it looked as if someone had been stripping lead. The old oak door of the church was firmly locked.

'I don't see any sign of a vicarage,' said James. 'We'd better scout around.'

Nasty, dark, ragged clouds raced over the sky above. The wind whistled down the street, causing a newspaper to stick to James's trousers. He tore it off, and then, looking ahead, said, 'I think there's a little shop on the corner. We'll try there.'

The shop had iron mesh over the windows and a video camera slowly swivelling above the door. A very fat woman in a brightly coloured sari was behind the counter. They asked where they could find the vicar.

'Rand the corner, duckie,' she said in broad cockney. 'Number five. You gettin' married or sumpthin'?'

'No,' said James. 'Let's go, Agatha.'

'Did you know the previous vicar?' asked Agatha, ignoring James.

'His missus used ter come in here, pore lamb. I coulda killed them bastards what did it to her.'

'What happened?' asked Agatha.

Shrewd brown eyes looked Agatha up and

71

down. 'I gotta living ter make.'

'It is your civic duty...' James was beginning, but Agatha said firmly, 'Fifty quid.'

'You're a lady. 'And it over.' She tucked the note somewhere in her capacious bosom. 'It were last year. The Gorley Street gang caught 'er on 'er road 'ome. Raped the pore girl. Stabbed 'er. Left 'er for dead. But 'er was seen by a chap in a motor. Called the ambulance and the perlice. They rounded up the gang. Judge threw the book at them.'

'I found nothing about this on the internet,' said James.

''Er 'usband 'ad some powerful friends, or so I 'card, and they gets on to the newspapers and makes sure the wife's name isn't mentioned.'

Agatha thanked her and was about to leave the amazingly well-stocked shop when she saw a refrigerator case with jam doughnuts on offer.

'We haven't time for that,' snapped James as Agatha opened the door and appeared to fall into a trance-like state.

'Shut up,' said Agatha. She selected six and put them in a cardboard box and then paid for them.

The wind seemed to have increased in ferocity and moaned through the deserted building like some banshee heralding death. The vicarage was standing alone in a vacant lot, the houses on either side having been cleared. They rang the bell and waited. A small microphone on the wall next to the bell asked them to state their business.

Agatha introduced themselves and then waited. There came the sound of several locks being opened and bolts drawn back and then a tall, muscular, brutish-looking man appeared on the doorstep.

'Are you the vicar?' asked Agatha.

'His minder. Come in. Ian and I were in the army together. Thanks for the doughnuts. I'll just put them in the kitchen.' And to Agatha's dismay, he firmly took the box from her.

He led the way along a corridor and opened a door. The vicar was seated behind a desk. As they entered, he rose to meet them. 'I am Ian Ferguson,' he said. He had a light Scottish accent. 'And what brings a private detective here?' He was a middle-aged man with a thick head of white hair and what Agatha thought of as an ordinary face.

Agatha explained about the murders and how they wondered why the recent vicar had left and why he had managed to secure a living in the Cotswolds.

'I don't think I want to talk about that,' he said in a cold voice. 'Johnny will show you out.'

'We know about the rape,' said Agatha.

'Didn't you hear me? Shove off,' said the vicar.

'Yes,' said Johnny, walking into the room. 'And I am here to shove you if you don't go nicely.'

There was nothing they could do except let him usher them out into the windy street.

'Look, Agatha,' said James, 'we got what we came for. Let's find a cab, bus or Tube.'

'Maybe just ask that nice Indian lady...'

'No, you are not getting any more doughnuts,' said James.

'Oh, yeah? Well, you're not my boss,' snarled Agatha. She swung round and headed for the shop. 'Find your own way back,' yelled James. He stalked off in the opposite direction. He suddenly turned around, feeling he should not have left her alone in such a neighbourhood and saw to his horror that a youth was holding a knife in front of Agatha while another looked on.

Agatha said wearily, 'Let me get my handbag open.' She whipped out a can of Mace and sprayed both their faces just as James came pounding up. He took out his phone. 'I'll get the police.'

'No, you don't!' shouted Agatha. 'Run for it.'

She hared off down the street in her high-heeled boots with James running after her. To Agatha's relief, she found herself in a busy thoroughfare and across this main road was the entrance to a Tube station. James caught up with her and seized her arm. 'Why not call the police?'

'I used Mace,' panted Agatha. 'I don't think it's legal. Oh, poor Molly. I can't see it's got anything to do with the murders. There's a cab. Hoy! Taxi!'

'You are the only person I know,' James grumbled as the taxi moved off, 'who would hail a taxi to go and get jammed in London traffic when there was a perfectly good Tube station there.'

'Stop complaining,' said Agatha. 'I'm thinking. Look, would you say that Rory was the sort to have powerful friends?'

'His grandfather was the Bishop of York, his uncle owns the *Morning Herald,* and his mother is the Member of Parliament for Harrington. His father is a brigadier, Blues and Royals and his sister, Penelope, is married to the Duke of Hadshire.'

'But the establishment doesn't have any power these days,' protested Agatha.

'Just try crossing them,' said James. 'Look, no one, even in our slimy press, wants to be the bastard who wrote about Molly being raped.'

'Not then. But what about now when they're all reporting the murders and frightened the foreign press might get the story first?'

'You're too cynical. This cab must be doing two miles an hour. We should have taken the Tube. Oh, God!' James leapt from the cab, bought a magazine at a kiosk and caught up with the cab at the red lights and jumped in.

'How's your French?' he asked.

'Menu French, that's pretty much all.'

'Look!' James held out the magazine. Molly's anguished face stared out at them under a headline. 'What does it say?' asked Agatha.

'"From Hell to Hell. The Nightmare of the Priest's Wife."'

'Rory's not a priest, he's a vicar.'

'It's a French mag. Oh, that poor woman. She'll be mobbed by the press again.'

Agatha was quiet and thoughtful on the road home. As the train lurched over the points out of Paddington Station, she thought of all the times as a young girl she had dreamt that one day the miracle would happen and she would wake up beautiful and glamorous. In her old work as a public relations officer, she had only represented beautiful and famous girls. But most of them seemed to be destined to end up as arm candy, and then, like the trophy wives in the Cotswolds, started to fight a long and expensive battle with age, frightened that any wrinkles would land them in the divorce court. James had fallen asleep. He had loved her once. But what sort of love was it where the man laid down the law that you shouldn't work for a living and what to wear? The opposite was Charles who had bedded her a few times. An expert lover but a silent one. Not one word of passion had ever escaped his lips. He had once asked her to marry him but they had both decided it wouldn't work.

'What are you scowling about?' demanded James.

'Just thinking about Molly,' said Agatha.

'She's probably fled to relatives in Scotland.'

'I didn't know she was Scottish.'

'Educated at Cheltenham Ladies' College, hence the accent.'

'What does the family do?'

'Made a fortune out of slavery in the eighteenth century and then tea plantations in India and then railways. Hurry up. We're at the station.'

Agatha shook her head in bewilderment. 'I don't understand. All that money. She could have transformed that horrible vicarage.'

'They've only just settled in. And she's a woman, remember? She's got three brothers so it could be she only gets a small allowance from a family trust.'

'She wears supermarket clothes but I thought maybe she was being trendy. Supermarket chic is supposed to be the latest thing. You're making me feel I haven't been doing my job thoroughly, James. I didn't know any of this. Why on earth do you think she married a vicar and went to live in that hellhole in London?'

'It's called love, Agatha. Heard of it?'

'Once upon a time,' said Agatha. She closed her eyes and feigned sleep until sleep became a reality, only waking as the train pulled in to Oxford where they changed for the train to Moreton-in-Marsh.

Once back in Carsely, she refused James's offer of a drink. After she had petted her cats and fed them, she sat down and switched on her computer. Forget the murder of the policeman and of Mrs Smellie, if Mrs Smellie's death should prove to be murder, and concentrate on Margaret Darby. She had dumped John Hardcotte. Why? Did she try to compete with her sister? Her sister had been married three times and that was a lot to try to rival. Let's see, thought Agatha, a woman with a lot of money can get married easily. Maybe Margaret had been a romantic, always looking for the perfect knight. Think about that. How old did they say she was? Sixty-four. 'Sixty-four and never been kissed,' said Agatha.

'Who hasn't?' demanded a voice behind her, making her shriek.

'It's me, Roy Silver, Aggie. Your cleaner let me in and I fell asleep on your sofa. Doris knows we're old friends.'

Roy Silver had once worked for Agatha when she ran her own public relations firm. He was weedy and effeminate. Agatha knew the only reason for his visit was his craving for personal publicity. He knew of old that a combination of Agatha Raisin and murder meant plenty of press coverage and he chased personal publicity as fervently as if acting as his own PR. People like

77

Agatha might despair at what they saw as their lack of good looks, but every time Roy looked in the mirror, he saw a fascinating man. He was wearing jeans with holes at the knees and a denim jacket.

'What's with the retro look?' asked Agatha. 'Ripped jeans?'

'It's back. And the cheap look is in. Anyway, what about this murder, or murders? You've just got to introduce me to this vicar's wife.'

'You must be joking. She's probably fled the country by now.'

'But I simply must see this village. Can we go tomorrow? Pretty please.'

'Aren't you supposed to be at work? Wait a moment. Your employer has a difficult one and he sent you down here to pick my brains so you decided to kill two birds with one stone. Out with it.'

'Aren't you going to offer me a drink?'

'Help yourself and get me a G and T.'

With a drink on her desk, Agatha lit a cigarette and swung her typing chair round to face Roy. 'Don't dare say anything about smoking. Out with it.'

'You've heard of Pamela Forwith?'

'Who hasn't? Chain-store heiress addicted to la dolce vita. What's she been up to?'

'Someone sold photos of her to *Husky* mag. Three in a bed.'

'Are the men saying it's them with her?'

'No.'

'Right, get her on the phone and tell her to open an AIDS hospice.'

'Not fashionable anymore. Not now people are living and Bill Gates has given just this year five billion to AIDS research.'

'Decent men like him don't need creeps like us to sort out their scandals,' said Agatha.

'Think! You're not helping,' poured Roy.

'I've got it. Prince William and Kate and Harry are all red-hot for mental health support. Get her to open up a mental health clinic which will take the bad cases from the NHS and get a royal to be there at the opening. You got the photos? I thought so. Let's see.'

Roy passed the photos over. 'You can't really see her face, so the fly in the ointment is whoever sold the pix. Where did you get these?'

Roy hung his head.

Agatha gave a slow smile. 'You got someone to break into the mag's offices and pinch them. So what's the big fat hairy deal? Without these pix, the story's dead. Oh, oh. The photographer, yes?'

'The mag's not paying him and he's going to sue.'

'Where were the photos taken?' asked Agatha.

'At her Chelsea flat.'

'So he must have broken in to set up the equipment.'

'Maybe not,' said Roy. 'You can buy an alarm clock these days with a video camera in it.'

'That's an idea. Say she gets a present of an alarm. She might just put it beside the bed. Somehow the photographer – what's his name?'

'Barry Jinson.'

'Right. He calls the next day after the orgy after one of the men had let slip what was about to happen. Says the alarm was delivered in error. Apologies and all that. She hands it back and he's got the pix. Phone her up and ask her if she got any odd sort of present before the orgy and if someone came and wanted it back. Take the phone in the other room. I hate the sound of you grovelling.'

Agatha's stomach gave a rumble. She was hungry again. It was too late to go anywhere for dinner. Restaurants in the Cotswolds closed down at nine-thirty in the evening. Of course, they could drive out to one of the motorway places and eat junk food.

Roy came back. 'Hear this. She got the most beautiful antique doll delivered. She put it on a chair in her bedroom.'

'But how would anyone know she would put it there?'

'Either it was a good guess or the man who put this Barry fellow up to it was confident he could shift it if it wasn't in a good place.'

'Has she still got the doll?'

'No. It was gone the next morning.'

'Rats,' said Agatha. 'We have this unknown man to cope with. Did she know *all* these men?'

'One she didn't. Harold Peterson, some wrestler. He's gone off to the States, didn't know about it and the magazine never tried to contact him. The other is called Frank Aboty. I looked him up. Hedge fund banker.'

'What's he doing? What's he got against her? Oh, sod this. I haven't time to play unpaid detective.'

'I have,' said Charles, strolling in.

'This is not Liberty Hall,' complained Agatha. 'Oh, sit down and hear the story.'

Charles listened carefully and said, 'You haven't done your research properly, Roy. Aboty has a twenty-two-year-old son who was engaged to Pamela and she jilted him. Leave it to the expert. Listen and learn. Give me this photographer's phone number, Roy. Right. Agatha, there's a rerun of *The Bill* on. Switch it on and if there's a bit with police station noises, turn up the sound. Roy, the minute I tell him to call Scotland Yard, you dial a number on your phone, a number you know will just ring because no one's there and come over and hold it against my phone.'

He dialled a number and waited. Then Charles, in a broad Scottish accent, demanded, 'Is that Mr Barry Jinson?'

'Yes, who is calling?'

'My name is Detective Henry Channing of the hate crimes office. What? Oh, aye. Phone back. You've got the Scotland Yard number. That's just fine. I'll wait for your call.' He did not hang up at his end, however. Roy rushed up and held his ringing phone against Charles's receiver. Charles counted to five and then said in an Essex accent, 'New Scotland Yard.'

'I wish to speak to Detective Henry Channing,' said Barry.

'Putting you through.'

On the television screen, two policemen were talking against a background of ringing phones. Agatha turned the sound up.

'Mr Jinson?'

'Yes.' Charles mouthed *tape recorder* at Agatha who opened her handbag, took out the powerful little recorder she always carried with her and switched it on. 'Aye, well, it is like this. We have evidence that because a Mr Aboty wished to ruin the reputation of a certain lady, he colluded with you to take photographs of her in a compromising position.'

'It was Aboty's idea,' wailed Barry. 'Just a joke, see.'

'But you subsequently sold these photos to *Husky* magazine.'

'They've lost them,' gabbled Barry. 'No harm done. Look, it was a joke. I promise neither of us will contact or go near her again.'

'We'll maybe have to take your word for it, laddie. Let me be having a wee word with my boss. Miss Pamela has been fairly generous to our Widows and Orphans Charity. I'll be calling you back.'

Charles rang off. 'Let's see if that works. What's happening with your murders, Agatha?'

'Nothing so far,' said Agatha, deciding not to talk about the rape of the vicar's wife in front of Roy. Roy knew so many people and Roy gossiped. 'I'm hungry. Anyone fancy going out to a greasy spoon on the nearest motorway?'

'I've eaten,' said Charles, 'but I'll come with you and have a coffee.'

'Actually, I could murder an all-day breakfast,' said Roy.

As they were getting their coats on, Roy's mobile rang. He turned a whiter shade of pale and shot out of the room, saying, 'Oh, God. It's her!'

Agatha and Charles waited. 'Why does he do it?' asked Charles. 'Public relations, I mean. He's always rushing to you for help.'

'He's in love with publicity and he's in love with famous people. PR gives him a foot in the door.'

'Maybe we should take our coats off,' said Charles.

They waited anxiously. Finally Roy came back, looking radiant. 'That was Pamela. Barry phoned her up in tears and swore on so many Bibles that no one is talking. I told her how I masqueraded as a Scotland Yard detective. She says I am the most brilliant man in the world to think up such a trick. And I told her my idea of opening a mental health clinic so as to give her a Princess Di profile and she said I was so wonderful that I have to handle all her publicity in the future. So, my darlings, I am going back to London pronto. Sometimes my sheer cleverness amazes me!'

'Actually, it was my trick,' said Charles. 'Sometimes your barefaced cheek amazes me!'

'I could hardly tell her I'd been talking to friends about her sex life, now, could I? I think I'd better go back to London,' said Roy.

Agatha and Charles headed for a restaurant called The Burger Basement on the nearest ring road. It wasn't in a basement but someone had thought up the name and found it good. Agatha wolfed down a cheeseburger and fries. 'I really must go on a diet,' she sighed.

'Exercise is the thing. I thought you were going to a Pilates class.'

'I was. The trouble was I felt so noble after each

83

session that I rewarded myself with chocolate.'

'So let's get back to the case in hand,' said Charles. 'The vicar seems to have pulled a lot of strings to keep his wife's case out of the papers. So say Margaret Darby finds out. Maybe she's jealous of Molly's beauty and taunts her with it. That policeman finds the evidence when he's snooping around her house and so he has to go as well.'

'The one thing against that theory is the death of Mrs Smellie. My money's on some sort of lover who was after her money. What if the sister doesn't inherit? I'll get Patrick to find out the name of her lawyer.'

'We could just go and ask her. Where does she live?'

'Don't know. I do know she's called Laura Darby. Patrick said she came in to talk to Wilkes and then stayed at the George which means she can't be local. I'll call Patrick.'

Patrick said he had found her address in Oxford. Number four, Bentley Lane in Jericho. 'Why is it called Jericho?' Agatha asked, after she had rung off.

'It used to be outside the city walls where travellers rested. So they say that's how it got its name. Anyway, it was a red-light district in the fifties and the whole place was nearly demolished, but the preservationists saved it and now it's des res. I'll come with you, or is James going?'

'No, I didn't ask him.'

'It's late. Get me back to my car and I'll see you at what? Nine?'

'Fine,' said Agatha.

Chapter Six

'Will the sun never shine again?' mourned Agatha as she cruised along Walton Street in Oxford. Her windscreen was smeared with a greasy drizzle. Brown autumn leaves swirled in front of the car, blown by a gusty wind. 'We should be nearly there.'

'There! Turn right,' ordered Charles. 'You must be the last person in the world who doesn't have a sat-nav.'

'It's all that technical guff,' protested Agatha. 'Maybe next year. Here we are. You park this damned thing. That space is too small.'

'That space is big enough for a flatbed truck,' said Charles. 'Oh, don't glower. I'll do it.'

Agatha turned her head away as Charles efficiently parked her car. She hated people parking the car for her. They always looked so smug. She looked instead at the two-up two-down house where Laura lived. No garden at the front. Originally a worker's cottage. Cheap brick, north facing, probably damp. Fashion was an amazing thing, reflected Agatha, when someone as rich as Laura should choose to live in a dump like this.

When Charles joined her Agatha said, 'There's a sign there. It's residents' parking only.'

'I'm sure we'll be out of here before they catch us.'

Agatha rang the bell in a box on the wall beside

the red painted door.

Above the bell, a camera swivelled to look down at them. 'Who are you?' demanded a tinny voice from the bell box.

'Agatha Raisin, private detective, and Sir Charles Fraith.'

'Well, you can just push... Did you say Charles Fraith?'

'Yes.'

'Wait a minute!'

Rattle of locks being opened before the door swung open. 'Why, it is you, Sir Charles,' cooed Laura. 'I went to your fête last year. Such a pity about the rain. Do come in to my humble abode.' Ignoring Agatha, she seized Charles by the arm as if arresting him.

'We'll talk in my little sanctum,' she said, propelling Charles into a front room and shutting the door on Agatha. To Charles's surprise, Agatha didn't open the door and follow them in. Laura's 'sanctum' looked like a stage set. Bookshelves of hardback books lined one wall, all the covers still bright and new. A painting of a green and orange nude was hung over the fireplace which did not boast a fire but an arrangement of pine-cones painted silver. Tables and whatnots were covered with framed photographs of Laura at different points in her life. There was, however, one stylish piece of what Charles at first took to be modem sculpture until it dawned on him it was a Dyson heater looking like a piece by Henry Moore.

'Do sit down,' gushed Laura. 'A leetle sherry?'

'No, I'm fine. We wanted to know if your sister had any beau other than John Hardcotte.'

'Not that I know of, but she did *hint*. She was always hinting that some man was desperately in love with her. Poor Margaret. She was quite smitten with the new vicar until she saw his wife. Can't compete with that! Then she was always haunting Sir Edward's place until his wife told her to go away, although one could compete with *her*. Sir Edward, poor man, is quite dotty. I believe something nasty happened to him in the jungle.'

'Amazing,' said Charles. 'You live here and yet you seem to have picked up an enormous fund of gossip about Sumpton Harcourt.'

'I used to visit Margaret until recently when she went all funny about my diamond brooch. Said Mother had left it to her. Rubbish! Said she wanted to wear it on her wedding day. I asked her what she was talking about and what wedding and she did that silly wouldn't-you-like-to-know smirk of hers. Poor deluded Margaret. She was always fancying herself in love with this or that. But usually it was someone unobtainable. Then she could dream without really having to *commit*.'

Charles was seated in an armchair beside the fireplace. 'Now,' she said, 'little me has no trouble at all in committing to all sorts of naughty, *naughty* things.' To Charles's horror, she rose swiftly from the sofa, crossed the room and perched on the arm of his chair.

He leapt to his feet, nearly knocking her over. 'Good gracious. Is that the time? Such good company, I quite forgot I have to see my bank manager.'

He fled from the room and out into the windy

street to find Agatha behind the wheel placidly smoking a cigarette. 'Drive on,' ordered Charles, getting into the passenger seat.

'Tried to seduce you, I'll bet,' said Agatha, scraping the side of her car on a lamppost.

'You've just scraped your car!' shouted Charles.

'I know. What a relief. The trouble with having a new car is one always frets about when the first awful scratch is going to be. Now it's happened, so I don't need to worry anymore.'

'You are stark raving bonkers.'

'I am still a good detective. While she was waving her knickers at you, I had a look around upstairs. There are posters on the walls, like a teen bedroom. David Bowie, that actor from *Poldark* with the bare chest and Neil Oliver, that Scottish chap with the long hair. And on the bed are dolls and teddy bears. Yuck! She's mad.'

'Eccentric. Maybe. Look, lots of people have a thing about David Bowie, the *Poldark* fellow is all the current rage and Neil Oliver means she watches intelligent television. Did you see his documentaries on Scottish explorers? Brilliant.'

'The whole case makes me feel as if I'm wading through thick mud. You know what? Edward hasn't paid me a penny so I am going to tear up his contract and leave it all to the police for the first time in my life.'

'What if it turns out someone actually did kill old Mrs Smellie?'

'Oh, I don't know. Tell you what, I'm still quitting. I never thought divorces and missing cats and dogs would look so tempting.'

'I suppose it's only natural,' said Charles. 'I

mean, age creeping up on you.'

'Like to get out and get a taxi?'

Agatha was just about to turn into Beaumont Street and suggest to Charles that they had a drink at the Randolph, when he shouted, 'Stop the car!' He got out and before shutting the door said, 'I'll get the train back. Seen a friend.'

Agatha looked in the rearview mirror. A blonde wearing thigh-high boots with cruising-for-a-bruising high heels was just disappearing inside. She felt diminished. Agatha did not know that the person Charles had seen going into the Randolph was the tubby figure of Giles Mirfett, his next-door neighbour and prosperous landowner. Charles had a bone to pick with him about an encroaching boundary wall. Agatha did a U-turn, deaf to the infuriated honks of the drivers she nearly hit.

She drove grimly home. Despite a note from her cleaner, Doris, saying that the cats had been fed, Agatha gave them each a lump of chicken liver pate, made by Mrs Bloxby and certainly not meant to be wasted on cats. Hodge and Boswell. Stupid names. Hodge was something to do with Doctor Johnson about whom Agatha knew precious little except he was one of those literary giants Cotswold people quoted at parties. 'And sod them, too,' she muttered, patting Hodge who gave her an almost human glare as if to say, 'Can't you see I'm eating?'

The wind moaned in the thatch and rain pattered against the windows. Tomorrow, vowed Agatha, she would tell Edward that she was no longer interested in detecting for him.

The morning started badly. Dead leaves had blocked up a drain outside the kitchen door with the result that the kitchen had pools of dirty water just inside the door. She mopped up the water and went outside to clear the drain, forgetting to put a coat on and so got drenched by heavy rain driven in by a cold gale. By the time she set out, she was in a black bad temper.

Her reception at Edward's home was not what she expected. His eyes were rimmed with red. 'Have you seen her?' he cried. 'Where's Tiffany?'

She followed him into his sitting room. 'I've been up all night,' he moaned. 'The police have just left but they say it's too early to do anything about it.'

'Might she not have gone to visit a friend?' suggested Agatha, but her heart sank as she remembered Tiffany bragging that she knew the identity of the murderer.

'She would have phoned me,' he wailed. 'She didn't come home last night.' The doorbell rang. He looked out of the window and saw a television van parked outside and a man followed by a boom microphone and camera-man heading for his front door.

'It's the press,' he growled. 'I'll tell them to go away.'

'Don't do that,' said Agatha. 'We'll go out there and use them. Tiffany will hear about it and phone you.'

Agatha led him to the front door and opened it. 'My name is Agatha Raisin,' she said. 'I am working for Sir Edward here who is worried because his wife has disappeared.' Agatha propelled Edward forward. In a speech, he begged Tiffany to come home because there was a murderer at large. Then he gave a choked sob and hurried back into the house, followed by Agatha.

Edward was sitting hunched over on a sofa, his head in his hands. Agatha decided it was not the time to tell him she was quitting. But she was suddenly sure that Tiffany would turn up.

Later that afternoon, two village boys climbed the witches' tree after school and perched on a low branch. Carl Emery was eight, as was his friend, Joe Ash. Carl strapped on his father's headlamp used for cave exploring.

'They do say as how there's a gurt carp in that pond so I'm gonna shine a light down there and maybe we'll spot it.'

'I'm feart the witch might get us,' said Joe.

'Get out o' here,' jeered Carl. He had recently discovered that there wasn't a Santa Claus and this had made him bitterly reject the idea of anything supernatural at all. He fumbled with the switch until a powerful beam shone down into the murky depths of the pond. The pond was covered in choppy little waves caused by the wind.

'No good,' said Carl. 'We'll come back when the water's still. Can't see a blessed thing.'

'I can,' whispered Joe. 'I saw a white face down there.'

'Idiot,' said Carl. 'Mum says to bring you home for tea. There's apple turnover and cream.'

They scrambled down from the tree and headed off. Cable reporter, Sam Wherry, watched them go. He had been heading for the pub but had heard the boys by the pond and so had heard Joe's remark about the face in the pond. Sam Wherry was a dying breed – a real-life reporter of the old school who ferreted out stories where other journalists had given up. So he got into his car and drove to Mircester where he bought a powerful halogen lamp. He called up his photographer who had been sleeping off the effects of the previous night's binge and ordered him to hurry to the pond. He was lucky in that the television news editor had decided they shouldn't run Edward's plea until the six o'clock news.

The photographer, Chris Ramsay, had the hangover of all time and swore at having to wait in the rain and wind while Sam edged along the branch he had seen the boys on and shone his lamp down into the murky waters.

Holding the lamp steady, Sam peered down into the water. Like a flickering mirage, a white face stared up at him.

'Come along beside me,' he yelled to Chris. 'See if you can get a pic.'

'You'll need to move,' grumbled Chris. 'What am I supposed to be photographing?'

'I swear there's a body down there.' He backed off the low branch, Chris crawled along, Sam went after him and leaned round him to shine the lamp down into the water again.

'Get off me!' shouted Chris and elbowed him in the ribs.

Sam lost his balance, clutched desperately at Chris and both fell into the water. The pond was not all that deep. Sam was six feet tall. He found he was standing on something soft and shuddered. He bent down and pulled at what he felt to be cloth. But whatever it was proved to be too heavy for him to lift. Chris had gained the bank and was shouting that his career was ruined and Sam should pay for it, but Sam barely heard him. Sam got out of the pond and called to some of the villagers who had gathered, attracted by the noise, 'Get the police!'

Agatha Raisin was there before the police arrived because Molly had phoned her about the commotion at the pond.

The fire brigade was the first to arrive. Shivering Sam was given hot sweet tea and wrapped up in blankets because he refused to leave the scene.

'What's going on?' asked Agatha, approaching Sam.

'Please back off,' ordered the chief fireman.

'Agatha, I need a camera,' pleaded Sam.

'Got one in my phone. Here it is. Someone down there?'

'Saw a face. I think I felt a body. I...'

'Move away, madam. Now!' shouted the fireman.

'Talk to you later,' said Sam and he began to photograph the firemen from his seat in the back of a fire truck.

Although having ascertained from Sam that the water was not all that deep, a fireman put on diving equipment and eased down into the pond. The water only came up to his shoulders. So he bent down with his face under the water and the light from the lamp strapped on his forehead lighting up the murky depths. One thumb was raised.

Agatha groaned inwardly. I hope it's a suicide, she thought.

He called for cutting equipment and help. Another fireman suited up. To Agatha's dismay, Edward appeared at the front of a gathering crowd.

'Oh, hurry up!' Agatha heard Sam say. 'The others will be here soon.'

There was a gasp from the crowd as both men, who had bent down under the surface of the water, raised their heads as a body floated up, open eyes staring at the black, heartless branches of the witches' tree. The paramedics rushed to help Edward who had fainted. A television crew had arrived and much to the fury of the police, the scene was suddenly bathed in bright light.

Agatha scanned the faces of the watching villagers. There was a group of ten people, bunched together, seven women and three men, and their faces held an unhealthy look of suppressed glee. They were on the other side of the pond. One minute they were there, and the next they had vanished. The wind howled and two branches of the tree rubbed to give a groaning sound.

Agatha pulled her coat tightly about her shoulders. She decided suddenly to call on Molly. Where was the vicar? Surely he should have been at the pond to offer help.

At the vicarage, Molly answered the door. Agatha noticed to her dismay that Molly had been crying and felt a shrinking feeling of uselessness deep inside her. Other women might have given a spontaneous hug but Agatha's soul had two left feet.

'I could use a drink,' said Agatha. 'Could you?'

'Yes, I could. Come through to the kitchen. Mrs Castle has just presented us with two bottles of sloe gin. Fancy some?'

'Right now. Anything with a kick will do.'

'I haven't tried it. The kitchen's nice and warm. I ran out of Spanish brandy but it does well on Slivovitz. Sorry about the smell of paint. I was trying to brighten the place up.'

One wall had been painted white. 'Never say you're doing the painting yourself,' exclaimed Agatha. 'That ceiling is awfully high.'

'I'm nimble. Sit down. What's all the commotion out there?'

'I think they've found Tiffany's body in the pond.'

'I always thought her unstable.'

'No, the body was weighted down with something that they had to cut free.'

'Sit down, Agatha. That purple stuff's the gin. Help yourself.'

'I thought that was why you had been crying,' said Agatha bluntly.

'No, I've been getting nasty letters, or rather Rory has. They all say the same thing. I wasn't raped. I lead men on and then cried rape and so on and on and on. Last night in bed I wanted comfort and he shrank away a bit and then said he was tired. I swear deep down all men think women are asking for it. Pour a couple of glasses.'

Agatha, mindful that she had to drive home, poured a small measure into each glass.

'A toast!' said Molly. 'To hell with all men. Who needs them?'

'I wouldn't mind one right now,' said Agatha. 'Oh, someone to dream about and keep the world away.'

'What an odd woman you are,' said Molly. 'But I suppose you have to have a sensitive radar to be a good detective.'

'Was the rape awful?' asked Agatha and then winced as the fiery gin went down her throat.

'I don't want to talk about it.'

'Yes, you do,' said Agatha. 'I got that from Mrs Bloxby, the saint of Carsely. Mind if I have some more of that gin?'

'Help yourself. I never talk about it.'

'Never! You mean not to a therapist or victim support or Rory?'

'Talking makes it real.'

'Talking makes it go away,' said Agatha.

'Oh, really? When were you last raped?'

'Don't talk about it, then,' snapped Agatha. 'See if I sodding care.'

Molly poured more gin. The room fell silent except for the sound of the wind moaning in the eaves and hissing through the ivy.

Molly gave a little sob. Then she spoke. Agatha sat and listened, horrified. It was the beastliness of it, the insults, the filth.

'So that's it,' said Molly at last.

'Does it affect your sex life?'

'No, oddly enough. I think if I even suspected that Rory thought I had even a little bit to do with it, I would freeze up forever. Let's cheer up. Rory's brother should be arriving any moment.'

'Not a vicar as well?'

'No, he's an architect.' There was a knock at the

door. 'That's probably him now.'

'You stay. I'll go,' said Agatha. 'It might be the press.'

She opened the heavy oak door. A tall figure stood silhouetted against the blue lights of television crews. 'Are you the brother-in-law?' asked Agatha.

'Yes. Who are you?'

'A friend. Molly's in the kitchen.'

He moved past her. Agatha decided to go home. She needed peace and quiet to think. She longed to walk away from this case, and yet it was the worst one she had ever come across. Bodies everywhere and a village reported to have a coven of witches.

She followed Rory's brother into the kitchen. A strong draught up at the ceiling was making the single light-bulb sway back and forth on its flex. It cast golden lights in the brother-in-law's thick white hair. He was tall and he was handsome in a rugged way. He was the knight in armour, the *let me shoulder all your troubles* type of hero, thought Agatha, feeling dazed.

'Have you been introduced?' asked Molly. 'This is Guy. Guy, meet Agatha Raisin, famous detective.'

Agatha shook hands with him, feeling bewildered, then elated, then suddenly happy as if coming home to a much-loved country. Charles would have recognised the symptoms. Agatha Raisin's next magnificent obsession was upon her.

'What are you two tippling? Sloe gin. I'll have some of that. What on earth is going on in this village?'

97

'I'm tired, Agatha,' said Molly. 'You tell him.'

And so Agatha did, noticing as she talked that he did not wear a wedding ring, but then, a lot of British men did not. His eyes were amazing, almost like jewels. At first they just seemed brown but then she noticed they were rimmed round the iris with gold with flecks of pure green.

Agatha had just finished her tale when Molly asked, 'Isn't Annie joining you?'

Radiance left Agatha's face, like a light being switched off. 'I've got to go,' she said.

'Annie is history,' said Guy. 'You never liked her anyway.'

'Middle-aged women who think they are wild children are not to my taste.'

'Annie is forty-three.'

'That's ancient!'

Fifty-three-year-old Agatha winced. 'Only according to the Bible,' teased Guy.

Agatha rose to her feet and staggered slightly. 'Oh, dear, too much sloe gin.'

'Leave your car here and the keys,' urged Molly. 'Guy will drive you home. Agatha lives in Carsely. It's only a few miles away.'

'Delighted,' said Guy.

'Thanks for everything,' Molly called after Agatha.

'What was my sister-in-law thanking you for?' asked Guy curiously, once Agatha was settled next to him in his Range Rover. Agatha had no intention of telling him about the rape and so she said that Molly had urged her to look into the murders and that was what she had been doing.

When they got to Agatha's cottage, she saw to

her dismay that Charles's car was parked outside. She couldn't ask him in, Charles would say something off-putting.

But she brightened as Guy said, 'Let's continue this conversation. What about lunch or dinner sometime?'

'Lovely. Here's my card with the address of my office. See you, Guy.'

Agatha went into the house, singing. Charles came down the stairs wrapped in a silk dressing gown. 'You keep late hours,' he said. 'And your mouth is all purple. Been at the true and blushful Hippocrene?'

'Sloe gin.'

'And who was that I heard you say goodnight to?'

Agatha decided to lie. 'Just some copper. There's been another murder.'

'What! Mrs Smellie?'

'No, Tiffany.'

'Well, she did brag she knew the murderer. What was this copper like?'

'Who?'

'The one that drove you home.'

'Oh, him. They all look alike to me. I'm tired. Can we talk in the morning?'

Charles was about to ask who it was that had put the shine back in Agatha's bearlike eyes, but pulled himself up short. Only a husband or lover had that right. He turned and went upstairs to bed in the spare room. But he did not go to sleep immediately. He folded his hands on his chest, stared up into the blackness of the ceiling, and wondered why he felt vaguely sad.

Agatha awoke with a feeling of anticipation. This was the day she might see Guy. She had forgotten all about Charles until she went into the kitchen and found him sitting there with a gleeful look on his face. 'A chap called Guy Harris has just been here. Left your car. Says he drove you home last night. Doesn't look like a copper.'

'Charles, I was so tired, I couldn't remember who drove me home. And I have news for you. I don't want this case.'

'Not like you to be gutless, Aggie!'

'It's known as self-preservation. There is a mad murderer out there. I have been almost buried alive, almost chucked in the Grand Canal in Venice, nearly burnt to death and a lot more. I do not have nine lives. I want to stay alive. Geddit? I am going to have a strong coffee and then I am going to confront Sir Edward and tell him I am retiring from the case.'

'So that you can scuttle to the vicarage with stars in your eyes? Grow up.'

'Oh, bugger off, Charles.'

Agatha slumped down at the kitchen table. Charles studied her for a moment and then went to the coffee machine and made her a cup of black coffee. He slid her cigarettes and a lighter along the table and let the cats out. Silently, he went off upstairs to change.

Once showered and dressed, he was about to leave without saying goodbye when he stopped in the little hallway. What is happening to us, wondered Charles. Life would be very dull without

100

Agatha's friendship. He turned around abruptly and sat down with her at the kitchen table. 'Drink your coffee,' he said. 'I'll come with you.'

Agatha pressed his hand and gave a weak smile. Charles snatched his hand away. 'Enough of the soap opera for one morning. You look quite odd without your usual war paint.'

That had the effect of sending Agatha flying up the stairs to put on make-up.

Charles and Agatha found Edward being comforted by the members of the last dinner party. Despite her desire to get out of working for Edward, Agatha could not help studying them closely. Tiffany's aunt, Mrs Ruby Jones, had an arm around Edward's shaking shoulders. Judge Lord Thurkettle was saying, 'Courage old boy. Tomorrow's another day.'

'And it never rains but it pours,' said Bengy Gentry, and his sister, Brenda, added sotto voce, 'And inside every silver lining there's a great big dirty cloud.'

Everyone was drinking sherry, sherry being considered a suitable mourning sort of drink.

Edward had already begged Agatha to find the monster who had taken his beautiful wife from him before bursting into tears. So Agatha looked at him helplessly.

She said to Charles in low voice, 'Let's go and take a stroll around this village. I want to find out about the witches.'

Outside they found heavy rain had started to fall again. 'I saw a little shop as we drove in and it had a sign outside saying CAFETERIA,' Charles said.

'Funny about that lot drinking sherry so early in the day. I once had a nanny who sucked those sweeties, mint imperials, in church. She said God didn't mind mint imperials but would frown on chocolates.'

'I don't know anyone other than Mrs Bloxby who drinks sherry. I quite like the stuff, just so long as it's not sweet.'

They scurried from the shelter of the porch into Agatha's car.

The café turned out to be at the back of a general store. It had five tables covered in checked cloth and with old Chianti bottles holding candles, no doubt to give the place a spurious Italian flavour along with the posters of Venice on the walls.

A beaded curtain separated the café from the shop. A faded lady came through the curtain and lit a paraffin stove. 'Cold as a witch's tit in here,' she said conversationally.

Then she vanished back through the bead curtain.

A few minutes later, she was replaced by a young girl who had a spotty face and pink hair and a very large backside which she hung over the paraffin stove. 'What yers want?' she asked.

'Do you have any breakfast type stuff?' asked Agatha, realising she was hungry.

'Yes, mean eggs an 'at, like?'

'Yes.'

'Dunno. MUM!'

The faded lady reappeared. 'Them wants breakfusty things.'

'Like bacon and eggs?'

'Lovely,' said Agatha.

'Well, you ain't having 'em, see? It's tea and cakes or nothing.'

To Charles's amazement, Agatha said calmly, 'I'm not joining this coven if it has sour-faced old hags like you in it.'

'You was going to join us, like?'

'Not like, if it's full of people like you.'

'Now, now, don't you be getting your knickers in a twist, my lovely. Bacon and eggs coming right up.'

When the woman and her daughter had gone, Charles hissed, 'Are you out of your tiny mind?'

'I've decided to go ahead with the investigation,' said Agatha. 'I mean, there have been so many attempts on my life, you'd think I'd be used to them by now. I bet she wants me to join the other hags.'

Agatha flashed Charles a triumphant look as a seemingly delicious plate of eggs, bacon and fried bread was put in front of her. 'You be enjoying that there,' said the woman and went off wiping her hands on her apron.

Before Agatha could start eating, Charles snatched her plate and studied it closely. 'I thought so. The old bitch has spat on one of your eggs. See! That filthy globule to the side.'

Agatha picked up her plate and hurled it against the wall. Then she picked up the fat china teapot and sent it sailing off in the direction of the kitchen door.

'You daft cow,' said Charles. 'We could have called a health inspector. See where your rudeness got you? Come on. Let's go to the vicarage.'

To Agatha's disappointment, there was no sign of Guy and with Charles's cynical look fixed on her face, she didn't feel like asking where he was. And there was worse. Charles said, as Molly was filling the kettle, 'Stop slaving away. Let's all go out somewhere and eat junk food. Aggie loved the stuff.'

'I'm off food,' said Agatha. 'A cup of tea will be fine.'

'But it won't be fine for our Molly who longs to get out of here and stop making tea for every caller. Get your coat.'

'Did anyone ever call you a real Christian before?' asked Molly.

'I'm flattered.'

'Where do you want to go?' asked Agatha as they piled into her car. She kept looking around, hoping to see Guy returning.

'What about Harry's All Day Breakfast on the ring road?'

'Great,' said Molly.

'Would you like to leave a note for your husband?' said Agatha. 'Maybe he could join us.'

'Rory and Guy are off shooting pheasant.'

'Whose shoot?'

'Lord Thurkettle. He's not popular and he wanted to swell the ranks and so Guy and Rory get going for free provided they only take one bird each. Do you like pheasant, Agatha?'

'Yes, as a matter of fact I do,' said Agatha.

'Then you must come for dinner.'

'You'll need to hang them,' cautioned Charles.

'I've got a brace from five days ago. I usually allow half a bird each but I'm sure it'll stretch.'

'I'll bring you another brace,' said Charles. 'And what's more, they've been plucked.'

'I'd better get out there and do some detecting,' said Agatha.

'But we've only just got here,' complained Charles. 'I mean, you did come to see Molly, didn't you, darling?'

There was a sarcastic stress on that 'darling'. Agatha shifted uncomfortably. She had hoped to see Guy, Guy wasn't at the vicarage, so what was the point in staying?

'Of course,' said Agatha. 'Molly, are you able to get out? I mean, I see this village on television every evening. The world's press are cruising around.'

'There are even busloads of tourists,' said Molly. 'Some village bitch told the *Sun* newspaper that Rory was holding black masses in the church.'

'I bet it was that nasty cow from the shop-café place,' said Agatha.

'Oh, Mrs Fawkes. She's all sound and fury signifying nothing.'

'Until she spits in your food,' said Charles.

'Surely not!'

'Surely yes. I think it was because Agatha called her a sour-faced old cow.'

'I also said that I did not want to join her coven,' said Agatha. 'I just wanted to see how she'd react.'

'Oh, dear. I have just found out, there is a coven in this village and they even advertise their meetings in *Mystic* magazine.'

'I'll go off and find a copy,' said Agatha. 'Then

Charles and I can go to one of their meetings.'

'Go yourself, Aggie. Not the time of year to go prancing around in the nude.'

'After the reported bad publicity they got for that sort of thing years ago, I bet they keep their clothes on. Don't be silly, Charles. It'll be a laugh.'

He stared at her, his eyes blank and then said evenly, 'My time and my life are both my own. Furthermore I don't work for you.'

Agatha looked taken back and then she shrugged. 'You spoil me, Charles,' she said. 'I quite forget I have an office full of detectives. In fact, I'd better go and see what they are doing. Do you want me to drop you at your car?'

'I'll get a taxi,' said Charles.

'Don't worry. I'm going to call on Sarah Bloxby so I'll drop you off,' said Molly.

'I'll see myself out.' Agatha walked out into the dark, gusty day feeling strangely bereft. If Charles had been angry with her, she would not have been so upset. But it was worse than that. He had looked bored.

Agatha walked into the office. Only Toni was there, her bright hair shining under the electric light, switched on because of the darkness of the day.

'Any further forward?' asked Toni.

'No, but I would like to see who's in that coven. I believe they advertise in *Mystic* magazine.'

'I believe you'll find it in the personal ads at the back. We had one of those cases before.'

'Tell me honestly, Toni, do you think I take Charles for granted?'

'No. I thought it was the other way around. He uses your cottage as a hotel, drops in and out when he feels like it. James comes and goes. You need a man with commitment.'

'At my age, they've been committed already to some lucky woman, or committed to the loony bin, or committed to their own reflections.' She thought suddenly of Guy. Had he been married? Was he married? Molly was going to visit Mrs Bloxby, therefore Mrs Bloxby would surely know.

Agatha flicked through the personal ads. 'Ah, here we are. "Sumpton Harcourt" – why do all these villages have names like someone in a P. G. Wodehouse novel? – "coven will meet on fifteenth November on Hangman's Hill." That's tonight!'

'There's a Hangman's Hill between Blockley and Chipping Campden,' said Toni.

'Can't be. Not the sort of place.'

'I'll google it. Oh, they're all over the place. The best known one is in Epping Forest.'

'They've probably named some hill near the village themselves. I'll ask around. I'm off. Everything running all right?'

'Yes, I've wrapped up the Barons' divorce case.'

'Want to come with me? I got cold feet and wanted to back out and give Edward his money back.'

'Not like you, Agatha!'

'Wait until you start to spend more time in that rotten village and you'll get the creeps as well.'

Molly had left by the time they arrived. They settled gratefully against the feather cushions of the sofa in the vicarage drawing room. The fire crackled and Mrs Bloxby passed around tea and buttered scones. Outside the French windows stood the churchyard, the old stones looking as if they were hunched against the cold wind.

It was really only on television that people got buried in churchyards, thought Agatha. Cremation was all the rage.

Toni said, 'Agatha is wondering if you know anything about the coven in my village.'

'Funny you should mention that,' said Mrs Bloxby. 'I thought that had finished long ago and a lady in this village nicknamed Fiercely Puritan – I'm afraid my husband thought that one up but she is always complaining his sermons don't have enough hellfire in them and she does seem obsessed with sin – where was I? Oh, yes, well, real name Joanna Bentley says she has heard the coven at Sumpton Harcourt has reformed. And they are to meet tonight on Hangman's Hill.'

'Where's that?' asked Agatha.

'It's actually called Badger's Hill and it is just above the village. They did used to hang people there. There was a gibbet. But it's been called Badger's Hill for the last hundred or so years. You are surely not thinking of going?'

'Well, yes,' said Agatha. 'I want to see whether they are vicious enough to start killing people.'

'Oh, do be careful,' admonished the vicar's wife. 'I do think they take some sort of drugs. They used to in the old days. They rubbed something or other on their genitals and that gave them a feeling of flying.'

'I wish someone would rub something on my genitals,' said Agatha, and then turned dark red

108

as she realised she had spoken aloud.

Mrs Bloxby hurried from the room and Toni could hear her stifled laughter coming from outside.

'I think we should have an early meal,' said Agatha. 'It didn't give a time. What if it's at midnight? I don't feel like freezing up there in the bushes.'

'Tell you what,' said Toni. 'You go to the vicarage this evening and I'll ask around.'

'You will be careful? Maybe Simon could go with you.'

'No. Not Simon.'

'Why? Got a crush on you again?'

'No. But he's dreaming about someone. I know the signs.'

Chapter Seven

'Thanks,' said Molly early that evening as she accepted Charles's gift of two brace of pheasant. 'Funny how men are hanged but pheasants are hung. The niceties of the English language. Guy is doing the cooking tonight. He does waste a lot of streaky bacon.'

'I like to wrap the birds up in it and stick them in the oven,' said Guy. 'Can't be bothered keeping basting them. Oh, there's the door. Probably some journalist.'

'I'll get it,' said Charles. 'I think it's Agatha. I can smell French scent from here.'

'Are they an item?' asked Guy.

'Don't think so,' Molly replied.

Agatha came in bearing a large jar of cranberry sauce. 'Mrs Bloxby's offering,' she said. 'Evening, Guy.'

Charles was irritated to notice that Agatha was wearing false eyelashes. Then he was irritated with himself. Why shouldn't she tart herself up?

'You got a toothache or something?' Charles realised the vicar was asking. 'You're scowling quite dreadfully.'

'Bit of a headache,' lied Charles. 'Are the press still haunting you?'

'No, apart from a young chap who looks vaguely like Mr Punch. He lurks in the shrubbery so he can accost Molly.'

'He's rather sweet,' said Molly. 'I've finished peeling the spuds, Guy, you can put them on to roast. I told him to run along sharpish and stop bothering me and he looked so hurt, I told him to toughen up or he wouldn't be much of a reporter.'

'Amazing,' said her husband. 'Molly never notices when men have fallen for her.'

Must have a word with Simon, thought Agatha. I swear it's him in the grip of another obsession. Why can't he grow up?

She realised that Guy was looking at her and she suddenly smiled, not her usual crocodile smile, but a tentative, very feminine one that lit up her face.

Guy stared at her. Charles said loudly, 'Someone at the door again. I'll go.'

He came back after a few moments followed by Toni, beautiful as ever, with raindrops shining in her blonde hair. 'It's at eleven o'clock tonight, Agatha,' she said, shrugging off a scarlet puffa jacket to reveal a soft blue sweater that showed up her small high breasts to advantage.

'I think we should forget about it,' said Agatha. 'Thanks, Toni. No need to wait around.'

Rory said, 'Oh, she must stay for dinner. We've got masses.'

Toni looked uneasily at Agatha. Guy stepped forward. 'No one's going to introduce us so we'd better do it ourselves. I'm Guy Harris and I gather you work for Agatha?'

'Yes, I'm Toni Gilmour. But I feel I should be going. I promised Simon a drink.'

'That your boyfriend?'

'No, he's another detective. He said he was helping Agatha in his spare time by finding out as much as possible about the village.'

'Go and bring him in,' said Molly. 'It's a nasty night.'

Toni returned after a few minutes, leading Simon, who glanced at Molly and reddened.

'What on earth were you doing lurking about?' demanded Molly. 'All you had to do was ring the bell and say you were working for Agatha.'

'I thought you would have been bothered enough,' said Simon.

'Is there anything to drink,' asked Guy, 'or have you thrown it all on that wretched stove?'

'There's a box of Merlot on the counter,' said Molly, 'or there's sloe gin.'

How marvellous, thought Agatha enviously, to be able oh-so-casually to offer guests box wine and homemade tipple as well. It's all these snobbish

111

colour supplements and arty-farty TV programmes of the I-wouldn't-be-seen-*dead*-dahling-giving-that-to-meh-guests. They keep the class system going. In fact, thought Agatha, colour supplements and glossy magazines sometimes even have etiquette advisors. Who was that thin bitch who worked for *Super Upper* mag? Her conversation was limited to jeering at so-and-so who had cut the lettuce, my dear, or who had used a knife and fork to eat asparagus.

Guy found himself becoming more intrigued by Agatha as he watched her thoughts chasing like cloud shadows across her expressive face. But there was Charles Fraith, who was currently regarding him with a cold, assessing look.

Dinner was a pleasant affair and everyone seemed to enjoy themselves, with the exception of Charles who seemed on edge and Agatha who had become progressively gloomy. Did Toni always have to look so young and radiant? The men were laughing at everything she said although she was only telling a few stories about cases she had been on. Simon just sat and gazed at Molly.

At last, Agatha said she had better be going if she meant to have a look at the coven.

She got to her feet and Toni rose as well. 'That coat of yours is too bright,' said Agatha. 'Simon, you'd better come instead. Charles?'

'You don't need me,' said Charles lazily.

'Actually,' said Simon, 'I've got a bit of a chill. You could always phone me and...'

'Oh, forget it. Toni and I will manage!'

Outside, the rain was lashing down. 'They're never going to meet in this weather,' said Agatha, 'but we'll take my car and go a little way.'

They dived into the shelter of Agatha's car. She switched on the engine and the radio sprang into life. A pop group called Air Supply were singing 'All Out Of Love'. She eased the car in amongst the bushes and winced as she could feel thorns scratching the side of her car. Agatha jabbed the control button and switched it off. 'Quite right,' commented Toni. 'Don't want to listen to that particular song, do we?'

'Stop talking nonsense. Which way is this damned hill?' asked Agatha.

'Take the left road past the witches' tree. Maybe we should park a bit below the hill and get out.'

'I'll move the car further into these bushes at the side of the road,' said Agatha.

She eased the car forward into the bushes and then she heard more scraping sounds. 'Must be some sort of thorn bushes,' said Toni. 'Never mind. Your paintwork was scratched anyway.'

'Well, that wasn't my fault!' said Agatha with all the defensiveness of a woman who has actually ruined the paintwork on both sides of the car. 'People will keep running into me.'

'Maybe you should switch off the lights,' suggested Toni.

'I was just about to do that,' snapped Agatha. 'There is nothing more irritating than people telling you what to do just as you were about to do it. Let's go and see this stupid coven. Car's coming!'

They took cover by the side of the road. 'I

113

thought they'd all be walking,' said Agatha. 'But it's not like the city. People in villages don't walk. I swear my leg muscles have atrophied since I moved here.'

The narrow road was bordered on both sides by high hedges. They were just about to emerge from the shelter of these hedges when they crouched back. The road ended in an open clearing before the ruin of a farmhouse. Four women, dressed in black, stood smoking.

'Maybe we'd better begin the chant,' said one of the women. Agatha was sure she recognised that voice – the woman from the café. 'He did say he would come.'

They began to chant, their voices low to begin with but rising to become louder and louder. 'Come, oh lord, to thy servants here on earth. Rise from the pit.'

'Do they really believe this rubbish?' whispered Toni.

But Agatha sensed evil. The odd repetitive chant, the black night and the wind hissing through the branches over her head seemed to herald something wicked.

Then the farmyard became filled with purple smoke, twisting, circling and rising as the chant grew louder.

Agatha suddenly felt someone behind her and twisted round just as a syringe was plunged into her neck.

Agatha recovered consciousness at dawn's early light. She was freezing cold. Her ankles were bound and her hands were tied behind her and

114

she was naked. Above her, the skeletal branches of the witches' tree swung in the wind.

Two elderly village men were looking curiously at her. 'Mind, she don't have no stretch marks,' said one.

'Wouldn't mind a bit o' that in me bed these nights.'

'Untie me!' raged Agatha.

'Can't do, missus. Us phoned the perleece and they done say not to touch anything.'

Sirens sounded in the distance. Molly came rushing up followed by Guy and Rory. They were all carrying armfuls of blankets.

'What happened?' asked Molly. 'We're not to touch anything but we can throw these blankets over you.'

'Toni?' said Agatha. 'Did they get her as well?'

'Right beside you. But she's still out. There now. This is a cashmere shawl and it's lovely and warm and you can have my old fur coat as well. Rory, put blankets over Toni.'

A police car drove up and Bill Wong and Alice Peterson got out. 'They keep saying not to touch anything but we've got to get you both to hospital in case you die of hypothermia. Oh, here's the ambulance. Alice, if you would cut the duct tape and put the pieces in this forensic bag. Who did this, Agatha?'

'The witches were holding a coven and Toni and I were watching when we both got stabbed and ended up here. Bill, I'm sure one of them was the woman from the local shop-cum-café place.'

'I'll check with you later,' said Bill. 'I'll call on

115

Doris and get her to find clothes for you. I'll get Toni's keys later. She's still out of it.'

Agatha, who had passed out again in the ambulance, recovered consciousness in a private room in Mircester Hospital. She turned her head and saw she was sharing a room with Toni.

'Toni!' called Agatha. 'Are you awake?'

'Yes,' said Toni. 'Alice came and got my keys and told me we'd both been found stark naked under that tree.'

'It's all right for you at your age with your perfect figure, but what about me?' wailed Agatha. 'I'd got my legs waxed last week and bugger Brazilians, but I haven't been bothering about my armpits and they're like King Kong's. And that's how he saw me?'

'Who? Those old men who found us?'

'No, I mean Rory and his brother, Guy.'

'I don't think naked women give men lustful thoughts,' said Toni sententiously. 'If you had been wearing a bra and frilly knickers, that might have been different.'

'I want men to have lustful thoughts,' grumbled Agatha.

'Must be Guy,' mumbled Toni, thinking Agatha's found another obsession.

'What?'

'Nothing,' said Toni.

'Did Charles stay late?'

'No, Guy had to run him to his car.'

'What about Simon?' asked Agatha.

'He worshipped at the shrine of Molly but Guy sent him packing, just before he ran Charles to

116

his car.'

During the day, Agatha and Toni gave their statements and were told they could leave the next morning.

Toni noticed that every time the door started to open Agatha would pat her hair and arrange herself against the pillows, sinking back each time in obvious disappointment. She even looked disappointed at the sight of Mrs Bloxby.

When they were allowed to leave the hospital, Agatha ran Toni back to the vicarage to where the girl had left her own car.

'Let's drop in and see Molly,' said Agatha.

Toni shrugged. 'I don't want to.'

'Why?'

'We were assaulted in her parish. You are investigating because she originally begged you to. In fact, she very cleverly manipulated Edward into funding you. I think she might have called at the hospital to see how we were.'

Agatha hesitated. Then she said, 'Oh, well. I'm still shaky. I'm interested to find out what they injected us with. I won't go into the office today and you should take the rest of the day off as well.'

She took a last look in her rearview mirror before driving off. What did Guy think of her?

It was as well that Agatha could not hear the conversation going on inside the vicarage.

'Something very sexy about her,' said Guy dreamily.

'Oh, Agatha,' said Molly, pouring tea. 'Well,

you certainly got an eyeful.'

'Not her! The young one. Toni.'

'Back off, you old lecher. She's young enough to be your daughter.'

'I'm only in my early forties.'

'And she's half your age. There's another thing. Agatha has a maternal attitude towards young Toni and you certainly don't want to cross anyone like her.'

Agatha planned to have a leisurely bath and some more sleep. But the phone rang just as she was going to climb into the bath. She answered it and found to her delight that Guy was phoning her. 'Are you too shaken up?' he asked. 'I thought maybe we could have dinner this evening if you're up to it.'

'That would be lovely,' said Agatha as the fireworks of a new obsession spurted and glittered inside her head. 'I'll pick you up at eight this evening. See you then.'

Agatha had a hurried bath and then dressed and rushed off to a beauty salon in Evesham to be, as she put it, de-werewolfed. Her legs really didn't need waxing again, but she had them done anyway. She decided to keep her pubic hair, having read an article that men who liked shaved women were closet paedophiles. Every stray hair was plucked from her upper lip and her eyebrows were thinned. Agatha had always believed that the more hard work you put into your appearance before a date, then the more chance it had of being successful, despite the fact that she had been proved wrong, time after time.

Home again, she took out a scarlet cashmere dress and put it on and then let out a squawk of dismay. Her stomach appeared as a round bulge. She was about to decide to wear a body stocking when she thought about the hopefully undressing bit later in the evening. Time raced on and her bed became covered in discarded clothes. At last, she settled on a short black skirt under a long, tailored, gold silk evening coat, all worn over black hold-up stockings, French knickers and high heels. She was drifting down the stairs, enveloped in a cloud of Givenchy's Hot Couture, when she found Charles looking up at her.

At that moment, the doorbell rang. 'Shall I answer it?' asked Charles. Agatha would have snapped that she would open the door herself had Charles not added, 'You made the front page of the *Sun.*'

'What? Naked?'

'As the day you were born.'

'Got a copy?'

'Right here. I'll get the door for you. It'll be Guy ready to find out all he can about Toni.'

'It's me he invited out.' The doorbell shrilled.

'Told me he needed a few pointers about laying siege to Toni. Told him I'd break his neck. And you haven't looked at your post. There's a letter from the lab.'

Agatha walked stiffly down the rest of the stairs and took the letter he was holding out. Sitting down on the bottom step, she ignored the doorbell. She read its contents and said, 'No poison, no drugs. The old girl died a natural death.'

119

'Would you like me to answer the door?' asked Charles.

'No. Yes, tell him I'm ill and I'll call him. Gimme that copy of the *Sun*.'

Agatha stared aghast at the front page photograph. It showed Toni and herself, naked and tied up under that damned tree. Toni was still unconscious but the Agatha in the picture was glaring at the photographer. The headline was **BEAUTY AND THE BEAST.** It jokingly referred to Agatha's reputation for being rude and acerbic.

'I told all the journalists who were massed outside that you were still in the hospital.'

The letterbox clanged open. 'Agatha!' came Guy's voice. 'Are you all right?'

Charles simply shouted back, 'She's been sick. She'll phone you tomorrow.'

'Why didn't you open the door?' asked Agatha.

'Because of the way you are sitting. Stay-up stockings never stay up. One is crawling down your leg and you are flashing a pair of frilly knickers.'

Charles stared for a moment at Agatha's desolate face. 'Look, I'm off. Stop chasing the dream, put on something comfortable and have an early night.'

After he had gone, Agatha automatically did what he had suggested. She finally settled down on the sofa and switched on the television set, flicking through the channels and finding to her relief that an episode of *Endeavour* that she hadn't actually seen was showing.

She was just drifting off to sleep when Guy's

voice sounded through the letterbox again. 'Look! Just tell me you're OK in person and I'll go away. Molly is really worried about you.'

Agatha sighed and got to her feet. She went and opened the door. 'See! I'm fine.'

'I came back,' said Guy, 'to tell you the news. There's been an arrest. No, *four* arrests.'

'Come in and tell me about it,' said Agatha, feeling limp with relief and realising just for the first time how scary she found the whole business. She led the way into the kitchen. 'Coffee?'

'Yes, please.'

Guy studied Agatha as she moved about collecting cups, sugar and milk. She was wearing a loose black cashmere sweater and a black flared skirt. She had thrust her feet into a pair of scarlet high-heeled mules. She smelled of French perfume. The overall effect was sexier than her earlier outfit. Added to that was the fact that she was indifferent to him. An Agatha on the hunt could, as Charles once pointed out, actually cause shrinkage of the family jewels.

Agatha lit a cigarette. 'Oh, must you?' he asked.

'This is my house and if you don't like it, piss off,' said Agatha, 'or grow up and tell me who's been arrested.'

'Four women. Part of the coven.'

'Are they sure?'

'Yes, the four of them were actually photographed by a local dragging you out of the back of a van, stripping you off, tying you up and putting you under that tree.'

'So have they confessed to the murders?'

'I don't know. One of the policemen is related to

121

Molly's cleaning woman and she says the coven heard a wailing voice saying, "Come and get the spies". The ringleader seems to be the woman who runs the shop in Sumpton Harcourt.'

'That awful cow. She spat on my food. Wait a moment. My last memory is of a needle being stuck into my neck. They're still running tests.'

'So? What's your point?'

'I was watching them. Tired old bags playing at magic, that's all. Someone has already been trying to scare me off. All it's done is make me furious.'

'How's Toni taking it?'

'Quite well as far as I know. But a man of your age trying to get into her knickers has picked a bad time, I would think.'

'Do you have to be so crude? She is a beautiful girl and you must be used to men being smitten by her.'

'Yes, I am. My dearest wish is to see her settled down with someone of her own age. Goodnight!'

'What?'

'I said, goodnight. That means push off, get lost, *au revoir.*'

Guy turned and strode from the kitchen. The next moment she heard the front door slam.

'Why does Charles have to be right all the time?' said Agatha to her cats as she returned to the sitting room. *Endeavour* was just finishing. It was followed by the news. Death, misery, disaster. Agatha switched it off and went to bed.

When she awoke the next morning, she stared into the blackness and wondered again if the sun would ever reappear. As something rustled in the

122

thatch above, Agatha thought a romantic mind was a great drawback. Thatched cottages were great on the outside but very, very expensive to maintain.

Her uneasy thoughts turned back to the murders. It would be relaxing to know that the murderers had been caught, but Agatha did not believe any of the coven women were responsible. The police would have to release them. No forensic evidence, of that she was sure.

The phone extension beside the bed rang shrilly. It was a reporter from one of the press agencies asking what she thought of her experiences. 'I'm furious with whoever knocked me out,' said Agatha. 'What? No, I don't believe any of these silly women who play at being witches attacked me. They're just like small kids dressing up on Hallowe'en.'

No sooner had she replaced the receiver than the phone rang again. It was Edward. 'Harrumph, Agatha. Now that the murders are solved, I am terminating your engagement. As you have not done anything, I don't expect a bill.'

'Expect some for expenses,' said Agatha coldly, 'or I will take you to the small claims court.'

'Look here. I say.'

Agatha hung up on him.

In the office, she allocated jobs, saying, 'I've some loose ends to tie up and a bill to give you, Mrs Freedman, to send to Sir Edward. Toni, have you fully recovered?'

'Yes, sure,' said Toni. A junior doctor at the hospital was taking her out for dinner that evening.

123

He had curly brown hair, a good figure and he was only a few years older than she was.

Agatha's maternal feelings towards Toni were suddenly activated. The poor girl had been through a dreadful experience. 'Fancy having supper with me this evening?' asked Agatha.

'Can't. I've got a date.'

'Who with?'

'Agatha, just for this once, mind your own business.'

Agatha shrugged. 'It's your life.'

'Absolutely,' said Toni.

Oh, dear, thought Agatha. She always favoured older men. It must be Guy, that lecher. Well, he's going to be in for a surprise.

The day dragged on while Agatha, aided by Mrs Freedman, got down to yards of boring office administrative business. Toni arrived back from a divorce investigation and began to type out a report. Then the others came in and soon the office was full of the sound of clacking computers. At last, Toni applied light make-up and slung on a white fun fur.

Agatha reached for her own coat, planning to follow her but the office door opened and her ex-husband, James Lacey, came in. 'Thought you might like a spot of dinner, Agatha,' he said. 'I've just got back.'

'Oh, OK,' said Agatha, because James's handsome appearance always gave her a bit of a shock. His black hair was as thick as ever with just those traces of grey at the temples and his eyes as blue as the sea in his tanned face. But any resurgence of romantic thoughts were always dampened by the memory of his authoritarian behaviour: choosing her clothes and forbidding her to work.

It was when they were both seated in the George Hotel's dining room that Agatha remembered she had meant to look after Toni. She consoled herself with the thought that if Toni even caught a glimpse of her, she would be so furious, she might leave. Also, it was flattering to be entertained at dinner by a handsome man who was such a good listener.

When Agatha had finished, he sat for a moment, lost in thought, and then he said, 'I think you've hit on it. Or rather you had the right idea before this witch business. I think there might have been a man in Margaret Darby's life. Someone may have killed her for her money. Does the sister get it?'

'I suppose so,' said Agatha. 'I never really thought about it. I'll see if Patrick can find out.'

'Maybe the people at that dinner party know something about her. Lord Thurkettle collects stamps. I found what I think might be a rare one. Could use that as an excuse to consult him.'

'I didn't know you collected stamps.'

'I did as a boy. I was going to throw them away but a friend of mine said one of them might be rare. It's a one-penny stamp with Queen Victoria's head on it.'

'I'm not being paid anymore to investigate the murders,' said Agatha. 'On the other hand, it would be nice to hand all the grubby divorces and shoplifting and so on to the others for a day. So let's talk about something else. Where have you been?'

Agatha had not seen Guy dining on the other

side of the dining room because he was half hidden by a potted palm. But he saw her and noticed she was with an attractive man. The light shone on Agatha's glossy hair and her face was animated. Feisty, thought Guy. Very feisty. He was dining with a male friend, having been turned down by Toni earlier. He had waited for Toni outside the agency and had asked her for dinner. 'Sorry,' she had said briefly and had rushed to join a very young man of her own age, making him feel like an ancient satyr. But if he bedded the boss and gave Agatha a right rogering, she might tell Toni and Toni would realise what she had missed. So ran his – very sadly – usual male-type thoughts. An amazing amount of men think a long night of Viagra-fuelled passion will make them seem giants of the bedchamber when in fact they leave the women feeling bruised and used.

James and Agatha set off to see Lord Thurkettle in their separate cars because Agatha said she might drive to the office afterwards. Above the bare branches of the trees, Agatha could see the pale disk of the sun. The village of Cuckleton looked pleasant compared to Sumpton Harcourt. There was a shop-cum-post office, a pub, a couple of gift shops and a restaurant called You Name It. Agatha supposed the cutesy name meant they could supply anything you cared to name. 'Turn right,' said the governess voice of Agatha's sat-nav.

Lord Thurkettle's house looked as if it had been plucked off the old airport road and put down in the village. The architecture was what was once described as Stockbroker Tudor in that it was all

fake, having been built in the thirties. The front-
age was gleaming white with fake black beams.
No thatch, noticed Agatha. Clever man stopped
short at thatch. Might get rid of my own and get
slate.

'What are you dreaming about?' asked James
who had got out of his car behind her.

'A slate roof.'

'Wouldn't that be great? I am sick and tired of
the upkeep and the expense,' said James. 'Let's
go.'

Lord Thurkettle looked as if he had been kept
away from the sun for too long. His skin was
white and powdery and his eyes weak.

James introduced them and said, 'I've brought
you the stamp to look at. Very good of you to see
us.'

'Why did you bring her? Oh, never mind. Come
in. Mary! Coffee in the drawing room.'

'Is that your wife?' asked Agatha.

'No, it is my daughter. You're that detective
woman. Poking and prying. Sit down! Not you,
Lacey. Bring the stamp over to the light. Mmm.
Victorian penny stamp with postmark and envelope. Not bad. Won't get you a fortune. About
three hundred and fifty pounds at best. That's all.
Let me show you some of my best ones.'

They both sat down at a large mahogany desk
while Agatha sat, forgotten.

In these DNA days when so many crimes were
being solved by forensics, Agatha often felt like a
dinosaur. But a lot of her success was due to her
sharp intuition. Governments had experienced

intelligence failures in the past due to over-reliance on satellites and forgetting a man on the ground could be much more useful. And so, while the police often concentrated too much on technology and waiting months for DNA results, Agatha ferreted, looked and assessed. So instead of trying to butt in as she would have done not so long ago, Agatha sat quietly and studied Lord Thurkettle. She had read up on him before leaving her home. He had spent some time in the Army before studying for the law. Wife deceased. One daughter. No scandal. No bad vibes.

Lord Thurkettle suddenly looked round. 'The Irish would call you a mind fecker, Mrs Raisin. I can almost feel you scrabbling about in my brain. Stop it. I have not murdered anyone. Read a magazine.'

Creepy, thought Agatha. But Patrick had told her that some detectives and policemen developed a sort of radar that could zoom into some villain's head and tell whether he was lying or not. She picked up a copy of *Cotswold Life* from the coffee table in front of her and began to read a soothing article about a lavender farm.

Both men joined her as Mary entered pushing a trolley laded with coffeepot, cups and biscuits.

'My apologies, Mrs Raisin. I hope I did not offend you.'

'No, because I'm curious. If you have developed a sort of sixth sense, perhaps you have an idea about who killed Margaret Darby?'

'It might be an idea to start at the middle,' he said.

'The middle of what?'

'I heard you had been concentrating on poor Margaret Darby. What about concentrating on Tiffany? She bragged about knowing the identity of the murderer and I am sure you, like me, thought she was lying. But the murderer didn't. So who? Start asking her husband about her friends. She was supposed to go to London to visit friends, was she not? What friends? Did she say anything to them? She obviously did not leave but she may have said something if she phoned them to put off her visit.'

'The sad fact is that I have to work for a living,' said Agatha, 'and Edward has cancelled his contract with me.'

'Don't look hopefully at me,' said the old judge. 'Ageing is frightfully expensive. I shall soon need nurses to wipe the drool from my senile lips.'

After they had left and were standing outside, Agatha said, 'Let's find a pub and I'll phone Patrick. I'm sure the police have the name of the friend that Tiffany was staying with.'

'What about the one in Sumpton Harcourt?'

'No, I'd rather try the one here. Maybe if we went to that damned witches' village someone would stick a needle in my neck again.'

The village pub was called the King Charles and there was a bad painting of His Majesty swinging in the wind outside.

The brewery which owned the pub had attempted to make it cosy but a thick carpet of yellow and red geometrical design covering the floor did not quite complement the Regency-striped wallpaper, or the paintings which were so amateur, James guessed they must have been painted by the villagers. Worse, there was piped Muzak.

"'I walked into the nightclub in the morning...'"

'James, what are you mumbling about?' demanded Agatha, sensing rather than recognising a literary quotation with all the irritation of the half-educated.

'I was quoting John Betjeman.'

'What's he got to do with anything?' she asked.

'I was prompted into quotation by the sight of that squashed tomato sandwich in the middle of the floor. Let's try somewhere else.'

But Agatha could scent gin, gorgeous soothing gin, sending out come-hither tentacles in her direction.

'No, let's stay. It's a good place to make calls. It's quiet.'

'Have it your way. Your usual?'

'Make it a double.'

'You're driving, remember? Only if I can run you home.'

'I'd forgotten it was still early in the day,' lied Agatha, but God forbid anyone would think she craved the stuff. 'I'll have a black coffee instead.'

Once they had settled into what the landlady proudly described as 'one of our new bonkettes', Agatha called Patrick to ask him if any more had been discovered about Margaret Darby's will. 'I gather she kept changing her will,' said Patrick. 'But she left it all to the Dogs Trust.'

When Agatha had rung off, James said, 'I thought Thurkettle's idea of concentrating on Tiffany was a good suggestion.'

'Yes, but I've got this nagging feeling that some-one might not have known that Margaret Darby had changed her will. I mean, the sister seemed to think she got the lot.'

Agatha phoned Patrick again and asked him to try to find out who the beneficiary was before the Dogs Trust.

This sort of pub is why people take to booze, she thought. What a dump! What filthy coffee.

'You forgot something,' said James.

'Like what?'

'Like who was Tiffany visiting in London.'

'If you are going to sit there and lecture me on how to do my job,' snapped Agatha, 'you'd be better off at home with your books.'

'You are only bitchy because you want a drink. You'd better be careful. You—'

Agatha's mobile rang. She listened and then said slowly, 'Are you sure?' She had half-risen to her feet, but she suddenly sat down again.

When Agatha rang off, she said in a shocked voice, 'In the will before sister and doggies, Margaret left the whole lot to Guy Harris.'

Chapter Eight

Agatha and James stared at each other. 'Let's think about this,' said James. 'If the man is that mer-cenary, then surely he would be chasing someone like you and not Toni, although Toni is gorgeous enough to make any man behave stupidly.'

131

'Like you once did,' Agatha pointed out, remembering the time James had made a fool of himself over the girl.

James got to his feet. 'And you are never, ever going to let me forget it!'

'Oh, sit down. I was merely retaliating. You pointed out that the only interest a man like Guy would have in me is my money.'

James stood on one foot, looking down his nose, thinking hard.

'You look like an infuriated stork,' said Agatha.

James sat down. 'So where were we?' said Agatha. 'If it's Guy, he may not have known about the change in the will. Maybe he needs the money. Or maybe she told him and he killed her in a fury. Oh, dear.'

'Oh, dear, what?'

'Do you think that Molly and Rory are all they seem?'

'They surely haven't been here that long. I mean for Guy to court Margaret enough to get her to change her will in the first place, he'd need to have been down here longer than them. Anyway, Patrick's coming to join us. He was on a job in Moreton so he'll be here soon.'

Agatha finished her coffee and looked at the plastic clock on the wall which told her it was eleven-thirty in the morning. That had always been the trouble with James, that puritanical streak. It had driven her in the past to say awful things to him. She gloomily ordered more coffee and flipped open her iPad. 'Let's see if Guy is here. Got him! He lives in Mircester. He's an author! I wonder why Charles didn't know that.'

'What's he written?' asked James. 'I've never heard of him.'

'That's because he writes as Jane Wither. They look like bodice rippers. *This Savage Knight* and about twelve others. But they're not in fashion, are they? Can't remember any on the bestseller lists. Oh, here's one and bless me I read it on holiday two years ago. It's a three-part family saga called *The Lancasters*. They had piles of it at the airport. So why would he need money?'

'Because he'd been published before. If he had been a newcomer up for auction at the Hamburg Book Fair, he'd probably have made a mint.'

'Maybe he got writer's block. So he arrives in Sumpton Harcourt *before* his brother. Maybe went to a village fête. He meets Margaret and sees easy prey. Oh, dear, I do like Molly. I hope they're not in on it.'

'Let's just go and ask him how he knew Margaret and see his reaction,' said James. 'Here's Patrick. Let's see what he has to say first. Drink, Patrick?'

'Thanks. I'll have a half of Hook Norton.'

They waited impatiently until he had been served and taken a sip. He took out a fat notebook and thumbed the pages. 'Let's see. Miss Darby changed her will to favour Guy Harris just about a year ago.'

'That's odd,' said Agatha. 'Rory wasn't vicar here then.'

'As I said before,' said James. 'Let's just go and ask them.'

Before they entered the vicarage, Agatha was again

seized by that odd desire to leave the whole thing to the police. In recent cases there had been attempts on her life and she was beginning to fear death.

Molly looked as happy and cheerful as usual. 'I made scones!' she cried. 'I'm getting Cotswold-ified. You should see with what an expert hand I twitch the lace curtains. Well, we don't have lace curtains but I mentally do it. Come into the kitchen. Guy is here.'

Agatha's heart sank. She had hoped Molly would be on her own so she could broach the subject. A direct confrontation with Guy might mean losing Molly's friendship.

Agatha introduced James and sat down at the kitchen table beside Guy.

'This is a sort of morning-afternoon tea. Help yourself to a hot scone, Agatha. You, too, James. There's whipped cream and strawberry jam.'

Agatha twisted her chair round so that she was looking directly at Guy. 'I could do with your help,' she began. 'You see, when someone has been murdered, I try to find out as much as I can about the character of the murderee.'

'So what's that got to do with me?' asked Guy.

'Well, you knew Margaret Darby very well.'

There was a long silence.

'What do you mean?' asked Guy finally.

'She left you all her money in her will before she changed it and left the lot to the Dogs Trust. It stands to reason you must have known her.'

Shock was registered on Molly's face. 'I didn't know you knew Margaret. You never said anything!'

'I am writing another family saga, sort of Trollope, vicars and bishops and all. I came to the church here as well as several other churches. On one of these visits I met Margaret. She chattered on about parish gossip while I mentally took notes. I even took her out for lunch. Then I realised she had a crush on me and backed off. I was doing a book signing in Mircester and she turned up in the bookshop and accused me in front of everyone of spurning her. She was delusional and quite mad. I was the one that encouraged you and Rory to come here. The minute I heard about Margaret's murder, I decided not to tell you because you had enough to worry you and that is honestly all there is to it.'

Agatha suddenly wanted to believe him. He looked so normal. No one could call Charles normal. Too mercenary. James was a confirmed bachelor. But somehow there sat Guy like that sturdy, reassuring man of her dreams. She smiled at him, a blinding smile which lit up her face. Guy blinked.

Then a cloud passed over Agatha's face. He had been lusting after Toni and what sort of middle-aged man lusted after such a young girl? The whole damn lot of them, thought Agatha gloomily, not realising that Guy was becoming extremely attracted to her.

Agatha's glossy hair shone in the electric light which always had to be on in the vicarage kitchen because of the ivy blocking out the daylight. She had a good, curvy figure and very long legs. She smelled of French perfume.

'Let's go,' said James abruptly.

Outside, they met Simon who was just getting out of his car. 'You're like a dog in heat,' exclaimed Agatha. 'You're supposed to be working on that divorce.'

'All wound up,' said Simon.

'There are other jobs to be done. Why didn't Toni give you something?'

'She's not the boss!'

'She is when I'm not there and you do know that because I've had to tell you enough times.'

'Leave the boy alone,' said James. 'Let's find somewhere for lunch.'

'I'll talk to you later,' said Agatha, but Simon was already ringing the doorbell.

Molly served Simon a cup of coffee and a scone. 'But you can't stay long,' she cautioned. 'I've got work to do.'

'I could help you,' said Simon eagerly.

'Women's work. You can't. In fact, you and Guy must see yourselves out.'

Guy looked sympathetically at Simon's downcast face. 'Molly's always rushing here, there and everywhere,' he said. 'What's your boss like?'

'Bit hard at times,' said Simon, 'but mostly all right.'

'Tied up with anyone? Is that James fellow her latest?'

'That's her ex.'

'What happened to cause the breakup?'

'*I don't know*,' said Simon impatiently. 'Why don't you ask her? Where do you think Molly's gone?'

'Don't know. She does so much already. Wait a bit. She's showing a film to some old-age pensioners in the church hall. *The Jungle Book,* I believe.'

Simon, as he walked to the church hall, planned to slip into the back in the darkness, just to be near his goddess.

But he walked into a brightly lit hall where Molly was dispensing tea and cakes. She scowled when she saw Simon and then her face cleared. 'Would you like to help?' she asked.

'I'll do anything,' said Simon.

'Take this tray of cakes round and see if anyone wants another one or if they want another cup of tea.'

Simon set off on his rounds, looking forward to the first order so that he could rejoin Molly. He was beginning to think no one was going to need anything when an elderly man said he would like another cup of tea. Simon bounded back to the table with the tea urn to find Rory, the vicar, presiding over it.

'Where's Molly?' asked Simon.

'If you mean my wife, Mrs Harris, she is in the ladies' ministering to someone who had a dizzy turn.'

'I was just helping out,' said Simon sulkily.

'Oh, good. Would you mind washing up the cups and saucers and plates?'

Muttering under his breath, Simon started to wash dishes while the wail of a siren drew nearer. Then two paramedics rushed in, followed by the fire brigade.

Simon turned round and glared at Rory. 'Shouldn't we be helping?'

'Relax. This is God's waiting room. We're used to it.'

Simon gloomily washed and stacked dishes on racks. Then he heard Molly calling, 'Going to the hospital, dear.'

'OK. Call me when you're finished.'

'I'm off,' said Simon.

Rory swung round. 'What? Oh, yes, well, thanks.'

When he was not determined to fall in love, Simon was a good detective because he was as tenacious as a bulldog. He planned to wait outside the hospital. He had noticed that Molly's little car was still outside the vicarage. So she would need a run home and he would be on hand to give her a lift. His sex life was healthy because there always seemed to be girls willing to go to bed with him. But Simon was a romantic and craved a great passion.

After an hour of waiting outside the hospital, Molly emerged looking to the left and right. Simon bounded from his car and then stopped still. For Rory was hugging his wife and she was looking into his eyes and smiling. Simon suddenly felt very young and silly.

He decided to go and call on Agatha in Carsely. But when he got there he was to find there was no one at home.

He retreated to the shelter of his car. It had stopped raining but it was very cold, with red and gold autumn leaves dancing down on a brisk northeaster. He got into his car and switched on the engine and the heater and then promptly fell asleep. He had gone to a disco the night before and had picked up an energetic girl who was training to be an Olympic runner. She had turned out to be as energetic in bed as she had been on the dance floor.

Agatha rapping on his car window woke him up. 'I want to talk to you,' said Simon, struggling out of his car.

'If it has anything to do with your pure and noble love for Molly Harris, I'm too tired to hear it.'

'I thought you might like to talk about the murders, but if you're tired...'

'No, come in. I, like you, could always do with a drink.'

Agatha bit her lip in vexation. Now Simon was hinting she might have a drinking problem as well as Charles.

To hell with both of them, she thought, as she settled down in front of the fire in her cottage with a large gin and tonic in one hand and a cigarette in the other.

Simon grinned. 'You are an insult to political correctness.'

'Sod political correctness. What did it ever do for anybody?'

'Well, for a start,' said Simon, 'it stopped a lot of people from dying earlier than they should have by shaming them into giving up smoking.'

'And closing down the village pubs and damaging the economy and having loads of old people cluttering up the wards who, if they had let them smoke, would have been dead by now. I thought you wanted to talk about the murders.'

Simon looked from the newly lit log fire to the colourful bookshelves and to a large vase filled with bronze-coloured chrysanthemums. 'It's homey here,' he said. 'I mean, no one would ever think of you as a homemaker. They would think of someone good like Mrs Bloxby.'

'And I am not good, you insulting little twat?'

'Sorry, Agatha. It started off as a compliment. OK, the murders. I read your notes. That voice that came down the chimney, any more threats?'

Agatha shook her head. The doorbell rang. 'I'll get it,' said Simon.

He opened the door. A man handed him a bunch of flowers and a large box of chocolates. 'Sign here,' he said. Simon signed and carried the flowers and chocolates indoors to Agatha.

'That's odd,' said Agatha. 'There doesn't seem to be a card.'

'I'd better get rid of these chocolates,' said Simon. 'They could be poisoned. And there could be something poisonous among the flowers. Remember that case where people died of wolf bane poisoning, something that can grow innocently in anyone's garden?'

'I've got a dustbin I use for burning rubbish down at the bottom of the garden. Throw the lot in there and set fire to it.'

Simon went off with the flowers and chocolates. Agatha was just about to light another cigarette when the doorbell rang. She went into her little hall and looked through the spyhole on the door.

'Charles,' she said. 'What brings you?'

140

'I wondered if you had found out anything more. Oh, this was lying on your doorstep.' He handed her a card. It said, 'Just little tokens of my admiration. Guy.'

'Oh, hell! The chocolates!' Agatha ran straight through her house and into the back garden where Simon's jester's face was illuminated by the blazing bonfire.

Agatha mutely handed Simon the card which he read by the light of the fire.

'Well, we've saved your figure,' said Simon.

'How did you manage to get such an enormous blaze?'

'You've a can of petrol in your shed. I poured it over everything.'

When they returned to the sitting room, Charles was stretched out on the sofa with the cats on his stomach.

'Weren't you even curious?' asked Agatha. 'I run screaming through the house to a bonfire in my garden and you show not the least bit of interest.'

'Elementary, my dear Watson. I hand you a gift card, you run off screaming about chocolates. So I deduce that you didn't get a card and assumed the chocs were poisoned. So where are we on our murders?'

'Guy is number one suspect because Margaret Darby planned to leave him her money before it went to the dear doggies.'

'Told the police?'

'They know. That's where Patrick got it from.'

'And where was Tiffany going when she said she was going to London?'

141

'Not found that out yet.'

'Isn't it time you did?'

'Don't get cheeky with me, Charles. I've got plenty of work and no one is paying me for this lot.'

Charles lifted the cats on to the floor as he rose and went to pour himself a brandy. He pinched one of Agatha's cigarettes and sank back on to the sofa. 'Have you tried asking Patrick?'

'I'm sure he would have told me.'

'He didn't think to tell you about Guy. Bit of a Lone Ranger.'

'Oh, I'll ask him.' Agatha rang Patrick and then looked triumphantly at Charles after she had listened and rung off. 'He doesn't know.'

'Bill Wong might know.'

'He'll never tell you,' said Simon.

'Listen and learn, my child. Throw me the phone, Agatha.'

Charles flicked open his own mobile phone and scrolled down the numbers. 'Why not use your own phone?' said Agatha.

'Because mobile phones are expensive.'

He dialled a number. 'Ah, Bill, Charles here. Yes, Agatha is all right, or rather I hope she is. She shot off to see that person that Tiffany was visiting before she got murdered. I'm worried she might be in danger. What? Oh, I see. That's funny. Sorry to bother you. No, I don't know how she found out. Bye.'

'So you didn't get anywhere,' said Agatha.

'Oh, but I did. She was going to see one of the fairy folk in Kynance Mews off the Gloucester Road. I know that mews. Not all that long. Let's go tomorrow.'

'I should be working,' said Agatha with a sigh.

'I'll go,' said Simon.

'No, I've got lots for you to do. I should tell James.'

'What's James got to do with it?' asked Charles, an edge of irritation in his voice.

'He helped me out yesterday. I think he should hear about the latest.'

'Suit yourself. You don't need to go there. Phone him.'

'It's just next door.'

The fact was that Agatha was beginning to wonder if marrying James again might not be a bad idea. She would not even admit to herself that she dreaded the idea of living the rest of her days on her own.

She sniffed the air. Smoke. Must be from the bonfire in her garden. But as she approached James's front door, she saw to her horror that it was in flames. She ran back to her own cottage and dialled 999, gabbling that James was going to burn to death.

'We need buckets of earth,' said Charles to Simon as they stood outside James's house. 'Look, there's a spade there. You start digging and I'll go round the back and throw things at his bedroom window. Oh, Agatha, get buckets. Chuck as much earth on the door as you can.'

Charles ran round the back of the house. He tore up clumps of sod from the back lawn and began to hurl them up at the window. In the distance, he could hear the sound of the approaching fire

143

brigade. He saw a half brick lying by the back door and smashed a pane of glass, put his hand in and unlocked the door. He went in and ran up the stairs and into the main bedroom. James was lying fast asleep. It was only when Charles shook him and yelled at him that he realised James had been drugged. James was over six feet tall and a dead weight. Charles tried to give him a fireman's lift but fell on the floor, cursing. He extricated himself and dumped James's body on top of a duvet and began to slide it towards the stairs. He figured if they could get out before the blaze from the front door ignited inside the house, they could be safe. Thank goodness there had been so much rain or the thatch would have gone up as it hung over the door. To his horror he heard a roaring, crackling sound from above his head. The thatch *was* on fire.

He dragged James's unconscious body into the bathroom and slammed the door. Stuffing the duvet under the bottom of the door, he picked up a jug and soaked them both in water. Then to his relief, he heard voices outside and the room was lit up with the lights from the fire truck. He sat down on the floor beside James, feeling tired and sick. He leaned his back against the bath and fell asleep.

He awoke and struggled as he felt himself being lifted up. 'I can walk,' he said crossly, and then smiled instead for it was a firewoman, a tall amazon with beautiful eyes. He remembered vaguely that there was some sort of health facility at the Fire College in Moreton-in-Marsh. Might be worth joining.

Then the dreary work of the evening began.

Charles refused to go to hospital but James was borne off. Statements had to be made to the ambulance men, the fire brigade, the police and then Bill Wong and Alice.

At last, Charles and Agatha were left alone. Simon had finally taken himself off, as had Mrs Bloxby and the villagers who had anxiously gathered at Agatha's cottage, reassured that no one was dead.

'Are you sure you're all right?' asked Agatha anxiously. 'That firewoman said she thought you were unconscious.'

'I fell asleep,' said Charles. 'It has always been my reaction to the thought of death. Look, Agatha, why burn James's cottage? Someone thought it was yours.'

'So who was up on the roof of my cottage that time, trying to scare me?'

'That could be one of the inbred morons from that hellish village and nothing to do with the murder.'

'But James went with me to interview Lord Thurkettle. Did you forget?'

'Never forget anything. Look, Aggie, why don't we bugger off to some hotel en route to London, get some sleep and then try to run this fairy creature to earth? Don't lose your nerve. Either we nail this bastard or your life is going to be in perpetual danger. Let's go *now!*'

Charles said he would drive Agatha's car. They stopped at a motel outside London. Thrifty as ever, Charles said they would share a room, but with twin beds, and Agatha was too tired to argue. She fell asleep almost immediately and was awakened hours later by Charles shaking her and saying, 'It's five o'clock. We've practically slept the whole day. Better chance of finding people at home in the evening.'

When they got to the Gloucester Road, a car slid out of a parking place and so Charles drove into it with a triumphant cry of 'See, there is a God!'

'So what's the plan?' asked Agatha. 'Don't you dare start asking for fairies or even homosexuals or you'll have the thought police down on us like a ton of bricks.'

'I bet he used to be an airline steward when she was a trolley dolly.'

'Honestly, Charles, no one could accuse you of bowing to the pressure of political correctness. So we know he's gay. That usually means he looked after himself. He may even be married so we'll go carefully. Remember, a good idea would be to simply ask if anyone knew anyone who used to work for an airline.'

Despite her day's sleep, Agatha was feeling weary again and her stomach was rumbling with hunger.

They were about to give up when, at the far end of the mews, the door was opened by a well-dressed woman in her forties. To Agatha's tired query of whether she knew anyone who had worked on an airline, to her surprise, the woman said, 'My husband. Is this about Tiffany? You'd better come in.'

Agatha made the introductions. 'I am Geraldine

146

Green. My husband, Clive, used to be a colleague of Tiffany's. Wait a minute. Take a seat. I'll get Clive.'

They sat down in a small living room, decorated with exquisite taste. Clive came bouncing in and Agatha wondered how on earth the police should think him effeminate in any way. He was powerfully built with grey hair and a clever face.

But when he spoke, his voice had a very camp Australian accent. Well, hello, Priscilla, Queen of the Desert, thought Agatha.

'Gerry told me what you're here about. But poor Tiffany never got here. She phoned from the sticks, quite hysterical and said the press were chasing her. I said, "I wish they would chase me, darling," and she screamed that she had told a lot of them, she knew the identity of the murderer in that quaint village and she needed to disappear. Well, my dear, do but survey my mansion. Couldn't swing a cat, let alone have a houseguest. So I said she could sleep in a cot bed in the living room for one night. But she never arrived. Next thing is Mr Plod the copper on our doorstep telling us someone has killed her. We were great friends at one time but she was one hell of a liar. I said to her, "Now you listen to me. It's no use going on about the family mansion when your accent is slipping into Manchester the whole time. You can't even say Manchester. You pronounce it Munchester." But when she nailed Sir Edward, I thought she was set for life. I assume she was lying but the murderer didn't think so.'

Agatha realised that she was not going to get any further. Tiffany hadn't even arrived. Some-

147

one must have waylaid her before she even left the village.

Agatha and Charles went for a snack lunch. 'Aren't the police supposed to watch their language?' asked Agatha. 'I mean, "fairy" is an insult, isn't it?'

'Yes, but it was said by one copper to an ex-copper. He might be lying, of course. But I can't see what reason he would have to knock off Margaret Darby. Unless there's some old Cairo connection we don't know about.'

'Meaning, Edward hired me to baffle the police? No, he hired me to indulge in dreams of being the great detective. Some of the time, he's not quite there. What a waste of a trip to London.'

'Needn't be. We could get a hotel room and make mad passionate love,' said Charles.

But Agatha was gazing through the plate-glass window of the café where the last of the autumn leaves swirled in a mini tornado on the pavement outside and was only dimly aware he had said something.

'I suppose James will have to move in with me,' said Agatha.

'Why? Surely his insurance covers temporary accommodation.'

'Yes, but...'

'Look, Aggie, grow up and stop living in dreams that maybe you and James could work it out. It's not going to happen. Come back to reality. Carpe diem!'

'Oh, crappy diem!' shouted Agatha. 'Let's go.'

Back in Carsely, Agatha learned from Mrs

Bloxby when she called at the vicarage that James had been given a temporary flat in Mircester.

Agatha settled back against the soft cushions of the sofa in the vicarage and heaved a sigh. 'Is the case getting to you?' asked Mrs Bloxby.

'It's not that. It's Charles. He's starting to become edgy and he's apt to sneer.'

'Give me an example.'

Agatha told the vicar's wife about her remark about James moving in with her and Charles's reaction.

'He worries about you,' said Mrs Bloxby diplomatically. She actually thought that there was a good chance Charles had been jealous, but to tell that idea to such a dreamer as Agatha would ruin her friendship with Charles. 'What about Guy? Are you sure he is innocent?'

'I'm pretty sure. There was a message from him when I got home asking me to give him a ring.'

'Why don't you do that? He's an attractive man. Yes, I've met him. If he is a murderer, that intuition of yours might suss something out. If not, you'll have a nice evening with an attractive man.'

'What makes you think he wants to ask me out?'

'He said something about you being a very attractive woman.'

Agatha glowed with pleasure. As soon as she got back to her cottage, she phoned him. He suggested she come to his flat on the following evening for dinner. Agatha agreed. But when she put the phone down, she regretted not having insisted meeting him in a restaurant.

149

The following day, Agatha gave Toni Guy's phone number and asked her to call in the middle of the evening to make sure nothing bad was happening.

Unusually for Agatha, she did not dress up. She was wearing a dark blue trousers suit with a white blouse and half boots in black patent leather.

Guy's flat was within walking distance. It was situated above a small Indian shop, still open, light shining on a multitude of goods. To her surprise, there were four bells beside the entrance door in an alley beside the shop. She pressed the one marked HARRIS and waited. After a few moments, the door swung open. Guy stood there beaming and smelling of vodka. I hope he's not a drunk, thought Agatha. How do you tell if someone's a drunk? They're the only people in the world who have convinced themselves that vodka doesn't smell.

He led the way up rickety stairs and flung open a door and ushered Agatha into what estate agents call a studio flat. It was comprised of mainly one shabby room, hair-cord carpet, vintage fifties objects and three chairs. It was more like student digs with a poster of Venice on one wall and a poster of singer Robbie Williams on another. A bookshelf by a gasfire was made up of planks on bricks.

'Sorry it's so poor,' said Guy. 'Alimony. Goes on and on. But she's getting married next month. Celebrations all round.'

'Because of J. K. Rowling, I always think writers are rolling in money,' said Agatha.

'Only four and a half per cent of the writers in the world can support themselves on what they earn. I'll be OK after the bitch's wedding. Drink?'

'Yes, please. What have you got?'

'Just wine. Got some nice Merlot.'

'Fine. What happened to the vodka?'

'What vodka?'

The answer to that is the stuff you are smelling of. 'Just joking,' said Agatha.

Guy went to a box of wine on the counter and poured a glass, handed it to Agatha and then stooped down and switched on the imitation logs on the gasfire.

'I thought it would be cosy to have a little supper here.'

Agatha looked at the card table over by the small window set for two. She felt claustrophobic. She felt trapped in a time warp of a student's room. She thought Guy had probably rented it furnished. The piles of books spilling off the bookshelves, she was sure, were the only things belonging to him.

'I'm surprised your brother didn't ask you to move in with them,' said Agatha.

'I did ask. But he said they wanted time together. I don't think Molly likes me, to be honest.'

Made a pass at her and got turned down, thought Agatha gloomily. And why is it that women like me have been schooled not to bruise the male ego? If only I could say, 'I really, *really* want to go home'.

Charles was walking to where he had parked his car in Mircester. He looked down the narrow

151

lane where Agatha had her office and saw a light shining from the window. He decided to go up and see her. But only Toni was there.

'I'm just about to phone Agatha,' said Toni. 'She's out on a date.'

'Who's the lucky man?'

'Guy Harris, the vicar's brother.'

'I'll wait while you phone.'

Meanwhile, Agatha was saying, 'Look, I'm sorry you're broke. Let me take you for dinner and you can ask me in the future when you're more comfortably off.'

Guy hesitated and then said, 'That's most awfully kind of you.'

'What was for dinner anyway?'

'Indian Summer Tikka Masala.'

'I know that one well,' said Agatha. 'Five minutes in the microwave?'

'That's the one.'

'I've eaten too many of those. Let's go!'

'There's no answer,' Toni was saying. 'Now, I'm worried.'

'Have you got his address?'

'Maybe. I'll check on Agatha's computer. She usually logs everyone's address when she's on a case.'

Charles strode up and down, waiting. 'Ah, here it is,' said Toni. 'Number 50B Swan Lane. Not far.'

'I'll come with you,' said Charles.

But they did not get any reply when they rang that bell marked HARRIS. Charles went round to the shop and explained that they were worried about his sister who was subject to epileptic fits and was on her own as Guy had gone to a book signing and, oh, please, did Mr Patel have a key? Telling a dainty creature in a sari to mind the shop, a worried Mr Patel hurried with them round to the entrance to the flats.

But once in the studio flat, they quickly discovered there was no sign of Agatha. 'Dreary dump,' commented Charles.

'Don't you go taking that tone with me,' said Mr Patel. 'It's cheap. Other people make it nice, bit of paint, but not him. I tell him, "Mr Harris," I say, "I tell you like the son I don't have. Keep out of that betting shop."'

'Oh, dear. My paws and whiskers,' muttered Charles. 'Where can the silly moo have gone?'

'He invited her for dinner so maybe they've gone to a restaurant,' said Toni.

'We could walk about and look in a few places.'

'You'd never make a detective, Charles. I'll go back to the office and phone round.'

At the office, Toni phoned several places without success while Charles put his feet up and read the local paper. 'Try this, one,' he called. 'It's a new Italian place.'

Agatha had been enjoying herself. Guy had told her amusing stories about a writer's tour he had done in America.

'I gather you suggested that Rory takes the vicar's job down here,' said Agatha. 'Poor Molly certainly needed to get as far away from the place as she could.'

153

'Listen. She asked to be raped. She *begged* to be raped.'

'What in hell's name are you talking about?' shouted Agatha.

'She flaunts herself.'

'She... Oh, for God's sake.' Agatha looked regretfully at her plate of spaghetti Bolognese for one split second before picking it up, standing up and tipping the contents over Guy's head.

The manager came rushing up.

'Get the police,' shouted Guy.

'I have pressed the panic button,' said the manager.

Charles and Toni arrived at the same time as the police. Guy was unlucky in that the police only that day had received a lecture on sensitivity to rape victims. He was also unlucky in that delighted diners had snapped multiple pictures of him covered in spaghetti. The manager was thawing rapidly. Agatha had promptly promised to pay for any mess. He had heard of the famous Mrs Raisin. He realised what great publicity it was for his restaurant and refused to press charges.

'I will then,' shouted Guy.

'Oh, I wouldn't do that, sir,' said a tall policeman. 'You said that a vicar's wife who was gang-raped *deserved* to be raped!'

Overcome with drink and fury, Guy burst into tears. The police led him away, saying, 'We'll get you home and you should go straight to bed.'

Charles ran Agatha home. 'I won't come in,' he said. 'Get some sleep.'

'I'll try. But I'm hungry. I didn't have time to

154

eat it.'

After she had let herself in, Agatha petted her cats and fed them and then rummaged in the freezer and brought out a packet of Indian Summer Tikka Masala. Irony, she thought, the gods are laughing at me. Oh, well, I can't be bothered looking for anything else.

But as she finally sat down at the kitchen table, her fork hanging over a plate of what looked like orange paste with lumps, Agatha had a sudden thought. Money was surely the motive behind the murders. Those witches had probably been released. Guy lived in poor circumstances. Had Margaret waved the promise of riches in front of him only to snatch them away?

Agatha ate only a few mouthfuls before tipping the contents of her plate into the rubbish bin. She was tired but was sure James would arrive soon. Forensic teams had been working next door in James's cottage. She decided to ask them when James was expected to arrive.

'Mr Lacey has been here today with the insurance people,' said one of the anonymous white-coated figures.

'So will he be back?'

'He said he had work to do abroad and now was as good a time as any even though the insurance company gave him the use of a flat in Mircester.'

Agatha let herself back into her cottage, feeling low. Somehow, she was beginning to be plagued with more feelings of loneliness than she had ever known.

Telling herself and the cats not to be such a

wimp, she showered and went to bed.

She was awakened by a strange noise at two o'clock in the morning. Agatha walked to the window, pulled aside the curtain and drew back with a gasp of horror. Five women were walking in circles bearing holly branches and chanting some weird unearthly song. Green smoke was rising from a brazier.

Agatha found to her fury that she was shaking. She marched into the bathroom and filled up a bucket of water, returned to the window, opened it and hurled the contents down on the singers.

'Ye be damned, damned!' they howled just as a police van drove up and they were arrested.

Agatha went downstairs to answer the door to a policeman who asked her politely if she wished to charge them with harassment. 'Oh, sure,' said Agatha wearily. 'If you've got to take a statement, come into the kitchen.'

'And, madam, don't catch cold. Better put something on,' he said, addressing the ceiling.

Agatha threw a coat over her mini pale-blue, silk nightie and led the way into the kitchen. The doorbell rang after a few moments but, to Agatha's relief, it was Mrs Bloxby.

'It's all round the village,' said Mrs Bloxby. 'Do you know these silly women are all members of the Rural Female Institute? Sumpton Harcourt used to be a nice village.'

'I'll just finish taking this here statement and then you ladies can have a natter,' said the policeman.

'Patronising git,' muttered Agatha, but fortunately in too low a voice for the policeman to hear.

156

At last he left. 'Come through to the living room,' said Agatha. 'I'm having a stiff drink. What about you?'

'Wouldn't sweet tea be better?'

'I'm sure it would but I want to sleep tonight.'

'All right. If you have any sherry, I'll join you.'

Agatha told Mrs Bloxby about her unfortunate dinner date and then about the witches. She ended up by asking, 'What causes it? Don't they know how daft they look?'

'They are usually on some sort of drug. I went to an interesting lecture about how the tale of witches flying on broomsticks came about. Rye mould is ergot fungi and ergot is similar to LSD. Applied with a broomstick to you-can-guess-where, it gives the effect of flying. I mean, people still talk about being on a high.'

'I wonder if I've been very silly,' said Agatha slowly. 'OK, to us they are a silly bunch of women, but I feel sure that could be really dangerous when they are full of drugs. I mean, they spat in my food. I should have reported them and got that café closed down, but I didn't want to get involved in long statements and so on so I let Charles persuade me to leave it alone. You see what I mean? I was already regretting charging them with harassment because I thought they weren't worth the hassle.'

The vicar's wife stifled a yawn. 'Better go, or do you want me to stay?'

'No, I'll be fine.'

Mrs Bloxby turned on the doorstep as she was leaving. 'I've just thought of something. Perhaps you should leave your cats with Mrs Simpson.

They might try to hurt you that way.'

Agatha repressed a shudder. 'I'll get Doris to take them tomorrow.'

Chapter Nine

The next morning, Agatha took her cats round to Doris. Then she returned home and packed a suitcase.

Toni arrived as Agatha was loading her suitcase into the car. 'Bill Wong phoned,' said Toni. 'He's worried about you. Says the witches were haunting your cottage last night. Are they mad?'

'Not that mad,' said Agatha. 'I heard one of them on the radio this morning. They feel they've become celebrities and can't get enough of it. So I'm off to stay at the George. It'd only a matter of time before the press start gathering in the village again. I feel hunted and hounded and Charles is a fat lot of use these days.' Agatha's eyes filled with tears.

Toni began to really worry. When had Agatha ever shed a tear over Charles before?

'You settle in at the George,' said Toni. 'I'll bring any stuff you want from the office. As Simon is still smitten with Molly, you could use this and send him to watch the vicarage. I mean, somehow all this seems to hinge on the new vicar.'

When Toni came back with the files from the office, Agatha was settled into a comfortable room which was unusually large, as older expensive hotels in the Cotswolds typically boasted rather small rooms.

Agatha ordered coffee for both of them and began to read quickly through the files on the murders. 'I think I should go and see that couple, Bengy and Brenda Gentry. They were at that dinner party and they were in the pub the day Tiffany disappeared. I've got an address for them. Fox End in the witch village. Did you send Simon to suss out what's going on at the vicarage?'

'He scampered out the door and roared off on his motorbike. Did Patrick have any interesting information?'

'Not much.'

'It is so annoying,' said Toni, 'not to have even a little bit of the power of the police. It's only on television that people tell the police to shove off. In real life, they turn a guilty colour and invite them in for tea. We don't have their forensics.'

'But we don't have all the other unsolved cases they have to deal with,' Agatha pointed out. 'When you've finished your coffee, come with me and see what you think.'

Fox End was a 'twee' cottage on the opposite side of the pond from the witches' tree. It was painted pink. It had plastic gnomes in the garden. The door knocker was in the shape of a grinning devil.

'We should have come here before,' whispered Agatha. 'They must be really weird.'

'I think it's a sign they are ordinary,' said Toni. 'Unlike you, I am not so far from the world of plastic gnomes. My mother loves them.'

There was a white bell push beside the door. Agatha pressed it. It tinkled out the tune 'English Country Garden'.

The door was suddenly thrust open and Brenda Gentry stared at them. 'I'm not buying anything,' she said harshly.

'And I'm not selling,' countered Agatha. 'It's me, Agatha Raisin.'

'Oh, come in. Discovered anything?'

She led the way through to the kitchen at the back. 'Sit down,' she commanded. 'I'll make coffee. You must try my rock cakes. They're famous. Rory says they are unbelievable.'

'Where is your brother?' asked Agatha.

'In his den. He's writing a book about the Sumpton Harcourt witches. He really should have had it finished long ago. We could have sold it to all those rubberneckers crowding this village. Could do with the money and that's a fact. Those damned unbreakable family trusts. I mean, you start off comfortable and no incentive to get a job and then living goes up and up and the pay stays the same.'

'You could still get a job,' said Toni. 'Train for something.'

'Got to look after Bengy. He'd be lost without me.' Her face glowed with a sort of maternal love.

'That night of the dinner party,' said Agatha, 'did you feel anything strange?'

'Only the effects of cheap wine on my stomach. Food was lousy as well and poor Edward has lost a few marbles.'

160

The door opened and Bengy strolled in. Toni thought he looked quite attractive with his thick fair hair. Agatha thought he looked effeminate. She wondered what it would be like to be married to such a man. Perhaps someone not so masculine as Charles or James would be better. 'Oh, yeah!' jeered a voice in her head. 'You could shop for gnomes together.'

'What did you think of Margaret Darby?' asked Agatha.

'Not a lot. She had a big crush on me and then she transferred it to the new vicar. Wouldn't leave Rory alone. "I'll kill that old bitch if she doesn't stop haunting me," he said. Ooops! Shouldn't have said that. But he's too attractive to be a vicar and his wife is a prick teaser.'

'You've got a dirty mind,' said Agatha coldly. 'I bet she turned you down and that's why you are being so vicious. Rubbish! I've a good mind to tell Rory what you are saying about Molly.'

'I was joking,' he said shrilly. 'I won't try to help if you're going to threaten me.'

'Sorry,' said Agatha, looking at him curiously. He suddenly smiled at her; a charming smile that lit up his face, and Agatha found herself smiling back. I wonder if he's gay, she thought. I wonder what it would be like living with a gay man. I wouldn't need to worry about all that sex stuff, shaving my legs, moisturising my body, all that lot. But he would want a sex life. Maybe someone like Bengy could turn out to be asexual. He's got a sort of androgynous face.

'Look, my dears, I've got to get back to my writing,' said Bengy. 'Why don't I meet you for

161

dinner tonight, Mrs Raisin?'

'Tell you what,' said Agatha, 'bring your sister along. What about that new trattoria in Mircester?'

'Just me,' said Bengy firmly. 'Brenda's got lots to do.' Brother and sister looked at each other as if communicating telepathically.

'All right,' said Agatha. 'I'll see you there at eight.'

'Scruff's order?'

Agatha looked blank so Toni translated for her. 'He wants to know if casual dress is OK.'

'Yes, fine.'

'I think we might have hit on something,' said Agatha outside the cottage. 'Let's go to the dreary pub.'

As they approached the pub, they saw Simon just going in and followed him. Agatha ordered a round of drinks and they sat at a table by the window. Outside, a pale sun shone down on shards of ice beginning to form at the edges of the pond.

'Who's been hacking at the tree?' asked Agatha, noticing for the first time raw white places on the branches.

'Souvenir hunters,' said Simon.

Then he turned a dark red colour as Agatha began to sniff the air. 'Sex!' she said. 'I smell sex. It's not me, it's not Toni, so what have you been up to, Simon?'

'It's your nasty imagination,' said Simon.

'Don't you see it's important?' howled Agatha. 'Guy said something about her leading men on. If a siren like the vicar's wife is screwing around, that could be cause for murder. What if Margaret

162

Darby knew something?'

Simon's jester face looked suddenly sad. He heaved a sigh. 'I just called in to worship at her feet,' he began. 'I know I was supposed to try to see if I could get information out of her but she was smiling at me and serving coffee. Then she cleared the kitchen table and stood up and looked at it. "I always wanted to try that," she said. "Come on. Get your kit off." It was brief and violent and afterwards she patted her hair and said she was off to do some shopping and just shut the door behind me. And so she went off, pulling up her trousers and knickers as she went.'

'She must be a nymphomaniac,' said Agatha. 'Does her husband know? I can hardly ask him. I'll sound out Bengy tonight.'

Agatha suddenly wondered about Charles's visits to the vicarage. Would he? Could he? Did he? She rose and went to the ladies' room and dialled his mobile number. He hardly ever answered it but this time he did and listened carefully while she told him of Simon's experience.

'Any time I was there,' said Charles, 'the husband was in his study or coming or going, but not by one flicker of an eyelash did she indicate any come hither desires. Must be losing my touch.'

'Tcha,' said Agatha and rang off.

Agatha dressed warmly rather than fashionably for her dinner with Bengy as the evening had turned biting cold. It was rare for it to be so cold in November. Frost was glittering on Lilac Lane as she drove off past the black shell of James's cottage.

163

She hadn't been eating much lately and her waistband felt comfortably loose and so she was looking forward to a great plate of pasta. Let the more sophisticated explore the delights of Italian cuisine: all Agatha wanted was a plate of spaghetti Bolognese.

Bengy was already waiting for her. He was wearing a blue and white gingham shirt, strawberry-coloured cords and a blue cashmere sweater. He had a rather camp voice and mannerisms but Agatha's sharp intuition told her he was not gay. There was a strong masculine streak there to counteract what he paraded as his feminine side.

After they had selected their meals and wine, Agatha started by asking him about the dinner party before the murder.

'It was pretty grim,' said Bengy. 'I mean, Tiffany seemed good fun but the wine was awful. It wasn't because it was box wine. I'm not a wine snob and some of the New Zealand stuff is okay but that stuff was sour and I think she'd added water to the decanter. Fact was, me and sis went for a laugh. They were so determined to be the squire and his lady, but it went past a joke. Edward definitely had a slate loose. You know, the Cotswolds are becoming like a theme park. "Find the Real Villager" should be a new board game.'

'I think the witches of Sumpton Harcourt could be classed as real villagers,' said Agatha.

'They're all bonkers as well. I mean, they could get a small fortune selling off their cottages but they make a good bit in drugs as far as I know.

Peddle them round the discos of Mircester and Birmingham. They make up potions and sell magic mushrooms, stuff like that. Charge a lot, too. I saw them selling their wares at Mircester folk festival, all dressed up like the three in *Macbeth* and people thought they were buying a legitimate bit of Olde Englande. I'm telling you, Agatha, in this day and age when the downtrodden middle classes are being taxed out of existence and you cannot make funny jokes about the Irish anymore and watch what you say and political correctness rules, you can sell a lot of people the myth of this green and pleasant land. Give us back our country. Send the immigrants home.'

'God help us if all the immigrants went home,' said Agatha. 'There would hardly be a medical expert left in the country. You were joking, of course.'

'Of course,' he said smoothly. 'Are your menu choices usually so unadventurous? Spag Bol?'

'Love it,' said Agatha. 'Now tell me all about Margaret Darby.'

'What's to tell? Spinster of the parish. Almost on the point of getting wed to a bit of rough over at Ancombe but sister visited him and he cried off.'

'Wait a bit. He said *she* dumped him.'

'Liar, liar, pants on fire. I swear, sweetie, it was that sister of hers. I know, because I happened to ask him.'

'Why did you happen to ask him?' said Agatha, her bearlike eyes suddenly shrewd.

'Was over there one day and ran into him and asked him when the wedding was to be. That's what he told me. Wedding's off.

'Asked him why and he said that Laura Darby had told him something and he wasn't going to go ahead. I asked him what it was but he wouldn't tell me. Let's talk about you. Tell me all about your adventures.'

Usually Agatha loved to brag, but she talked only automatically about a few of her cases while inside her mind was turning over implications of what he had said. Laura did not want her sister to marry the garage man. Laura had plenty of money but when had that ever stopped a greedy person from wanting more? Laura said she had inherited but she hadn't. It had all been left to the Dogs Trust. But had she known that?

They had reached the coffee stage. When Agatha finally finished talking, he said, 'What a fascinating woman you are. But you are going to be so, so mad at me because...'

'You've forgotten your wallet,' said Agatha.

'Oh, my dear, how too, too understanding. I must go to the loo.'

Agatha called for the bill. She noticed he had left his jacket over his chair because the restaurant was warm and was tempted to search his pockets, but decided suddenly to phone Patrick instead.

When the ex-copper came on the phone, Agatha asked, 'You heard the autopsy result, didn't you?'

'Which one?'

'Margaret Darby.'

'Told you. Strangled.'

'They didn't tell you by any chance that she was a virgin?'

'Funny that. They was making jokes about it at the morgue, calling her the Last Chance Saloon, you know, the last virgin in Gloucestershire. Anything else?'

'I'll call you tomorrow.'

Agatha settled the bill as Bengy came bounding back, still babbling apologies. Charles was always claiming to have left his wallet, thought Agatha, and experienced a strong flash of dislike for Bengy because he had made her think nasty thoughts about Charles.

They had only had one glass of wine each in the restaurant, neither wanting to risk being stopped by the police. Agatha was about to get into her car when she remembered she had run out of brandy and Charles liked brandy. She would not admit she wanted a drink when she got home. She walked to a small Asian corner store which sold liquor and there was Bengy, open wallet, paying for a bottle of wine.

'Evening,' cried Agatha.

Bengy swung round, his face flaming. 'It must have fallen down the lining of my jacket. Next time it really is on me.' He darted out the shop.

Agatha bought a bottle of brandy and made her way home, thinking that women who had money should never flaunt it, wear cheap clothes, and choose their friends carefully. The only good thing was that she did not have any relatives that she knew about. You can dump your friends, but relatives stick like glue.

'And talking of cheapskates,' she muttered as she let herself in and smelled cigarette smoke. Sure enough, Charles was stretched out on the sofa.

But Agatha was too full of new discoveries to get cross with him. As Charles took the bottle of brandy from her and poured two glasses, she told him about the odd contradiction of what the garage man had told her and what Bengy had said.

'We'll go tomorrow and ask him,' said Charles lazily. 'I'm tired.'

'What have you been doing?' asked Agatha, but all Charles did was drain his glass, kiss her on the cheek and go off upstairs.

Agatha sat clutching her brandy goblet. There had been a faint smell of scent coming from Charles's clothes. Who had he been with? She had no right to ask. She had no hold over any man on earth. And feeling almost pleasurably martyred, Agatha went to bed.

There was an awkward atmosphere at the breakfast table – and it isn't coming from me, thought Agatha. He's guilty about something.

'Stop it,' said Charles suddenly. 'I have a mild hangover, that's all.'

But Agatha sensed a woman. Mrs Bloxby would tell her in her gentle roundabout way to mind her own business. But Agatha began to feel old and dowdy.

The doorbell rang. 'I'll get it,' said Charles, 'just in case there isn't bubble, bubble, toil and trouble waiting for you.'

He came back bearing a large bouquet of red roses and lilies. Agatha read the card. '"Please forgive me and have dinner with me. Bengy." How nice!' said Agatha. 'Maybe he's not a real cheapskate like you.'

'And maybe he's a murderer. Stop drooling over those flowers and let's go.'

He waited impatiently while Agatha arranged the flowers in a vase before driving them both to Ancombe and to John Hardcotte's garage.

At first he stuck to his original story until Agatha said that, unless he told them the truth, they would need to report him to the police and say they thought he had been making false statements. If he told them the truth, then they would not go to the police.

On the corrugated roof of the workshop where they had found him, they could hear the rain beginning to fall. John Hardcotte sat down on an upturned oil drum and nervously wiped his hands on an oily rag.

'I was trying to protect her good name, and that's a fact,' he said. 'It was that sister, Laura. Her come over one day and says as how Margaret can't make our date 'cause she's sick and I'd better get myself checked out. I says, says I, "What's up, doc?" Jokey like. But her didn't laugh. Her says that Margaret has gonorrhea. I had to believe it. I mean, her own sister. So I told Laura to tell Margaret I didn't want to see her again and Laura made me write it down so Margaret would believe it. Her must ha' been right hurt.'

'Margaret Darby was a virgin,' said Agatha.

Agatha had read in books about people's faces being contorted with rage but it was the first time she had seen such a thing. His face became dark red and his eyes narrow. Little specks of spit flew out from his mouth as he snarled, 'I'll kill the

169

bitch. Everyone thinks I wanted Margaret for her money, but I loved her. I liked her being ladylike.'

'What do you think?' asked Agatha as they drove off. 'Oh, I'll drop you by your car and then I'd better go to the office.'

'I do think he was telling the truth. It's beginning to look as if Laura could be the murderer.'

'I don't think she would be strong enough to hoist two dead bodies up that tree.'

'Are you going to confront her?'

'No,' said Agatha. 'I'm going to watch her. If she had anything to do with the murders, then she didn't do it alone.'

'Right,' said Charles. 'I'm off.'

'Aren't you coming with me?'

'I have a life of my own, Aggie. Off you go.'

'And as one goes, another arrives,' said Agatha, rolling down her window. 'Hello, Roy.'

'I got time off,' said Roy. 'Thought I'd come and see you. Press around?'

'You'll find some over at Sumpton Harcourt. I've got detecting to do.'

'I'll come with you.'

'Oh, get in the car. We're off to Oxford. I'll tell you about it on the road.'

Roy only half listened as Agatha told him why they were going to Oxford. His boss, Mr Pedman, had wanted Agatha to sponsor a new miniature tape recorder in a series of television advertisements. Roy was sure Agatha would turn it down. He had suggested they get the lead actor from a popular spy series, but Pedman seemed determined to have Agatha. 'Best public relations officer the world had ever seen,' he would say, and Roy would try not to feel hurt.

'So,' Agatha ended up saying, 'you've got a boring day ahead of you, Roy. Why did you really come?'

'Ever heard the word "friendship"?'

'Out with it! What does old Pedman want?'

So Roy told her.

'Nope,' said Agatha. 'People on the road down appear in advertisements and I am still on the road up.'

'I should have driven myself,' said Roy. 'I could have taken the train. What a waste of time.'

'Oh, do shut up, you creepy little thing. Laura lives over there. I want to watch where she goes and who she sees.'

'Maybe she's not at home,' suggested Roy.

'Yes, she is. Saw her move across the upstairs window a minute ago. I'm hungry. Go and buy some sandwiches or something.'

'OK. What do you want?'

'Ham on white. And if you can find some coffee as well, I'll have a cup of black Americano.'

'Won't be long,' said Roy. 'At least it's stopped raining.'

Agatha waited. And waited. She wondered what on earth had happened to Roy. But Roy had hit gold. He had found they were filming part of the latest James Bond film in Gloucester Green. During a break, he had managed to tell the producer about the new tape recorders and how the Chinese firm would pay a substantial amount to have them shown, even for a second, in a bit of the movie. Roy had hit the big time. Mr Pedman

171

was racing towards Oxford and the CEO of the Chinese company as well.

The result was that Agatha lost Laura. She saw her leave but did not want to abandon Roy in Oxford. She waited hours hoping Laura would return, and by late evening she drove home slowly, finding to her fury that Roy had somehow got back and had taken his car.

She felt angry at having wasted a day. But if she waited for Laura to return home, the woman would probably just draw the curtains and go to bed.

It was at times like this that Agatha's faith in her ability as a detective began to waver. She usually saw herself as a ruthless, independent, modern woman. But all she wanted was some strong man to come along and take all the cares away. The feminists tried so hard. But was all this romantic nonsense hard-wired into women? It's because they have babies, you idiot, she thought. Babies! A son! If I hadn't been faffing around trying to make a fortune and be top of the tree, I could be going home to my family. Hard on that cosy thought came a darker one of a nagging imperious husband, making her life hell. Look at James. What a crusty old bugger he had turned out to be.

In Carsely, Agatha went straight to the vicarage and, despite a sour welcome from the vicar, was soon settled in the vicarage drawing room with a glass of dry sherry in her hand and a soft arm-chair beside the log fire. 'I've been feeling sorry for myself,' said Agatha.

'When there isn't a man in your life, you are

always sorry for yourself, Mrs Raisin. You need a dream.'

'Talking of dreams, did you never want a career?' asked Agatha.

'Of course. I was very ambitious. I got a first from Oxford and felt the world was at my feet. But I met Alf at the May Ball in my last year. And that was that. He was already the vicar here having graduated some years before. Friends brought him along. We were married three months later.'

Agatha wanted to cry out, 'What a waste!' but, unusually for her, remained silent.

But, then, the Mrs Bloxbys of this world from genteel backgrounds knew nothing of frowsy digs and hunger and driving ambition to do something, anything that would get you out of one of life's rat holes.

'Begin at the beginning,' Agatha realised Mrs Bloxby was saying.

'What? Margaret Darby?'

'Yes. Why poor Miss Darby?'

Agatha talked and talked until she began to see Laura and some accomplice as being guilty of the murders. Laura had shown that she did not want her sister to marry, and greed was a great motivator.

She explained this to the vicar's wife. 'Don't forget the witches,' said Mrs Bloxby.

'What? Bunch of silly menopausal women playing games?'

'They worship evil. Some man is probably using them. Or woman.'

'What do you know about Molly Harris?' asked Agatha.

'Only that she had a bad, traumatic experience.'

'Guy met me for dinner and more or less said she had been asking for it and that's when I tipped the spag Bol over his head.'

'Which probably means he made a pass at her and got turned down,' said Mrs Bloxby.

'No – as they say in Irish foreplay, brace yourself, Bridget, because this is shocking.'

She told Mrs Bloxby about Simon's adventure on the kitchen table.

When she had finished, Mrs Bloxby said slowly, 'Of course, it is television's fault.'

'Why?'

'No one would have thought of having sex on the kitchen table – so very unhygienic – if that scene had not been shown so many times on television and in films. I can imagine men who just wanted a bit of hows-your-father going on like that, but a woman would have to be some sort of nymphomaniac.'

Agatha gave a snort of laughter. She should have known that someone such as Mrs Bloxby would have seen it all and heard it all, and would not be shocked. People told the vicar's wife things they would not have dared tell anyone else. 'Could she kill to stop her husband finding out about an episode?' asked Agatha.

'I don't think so. Often they want to be found out and then abused.'

'This is the Cotswolds!' wailed Agatha. 'In all my dreams of moving here, I saw only sober, decent people.'

'Of which there are many. Another sherry?'

'No, thanks. I'd better get home to my cats.'

Charles was sitting on the sofa staring into space when she walked in. Agatha studied him, sniffed the air, caught that faint whiff of scent and said, 'It's always money with you. Who is she?'

'Patricia Brent-Arthurton.'

'Who is rich.'

'Very.'

'Beautiful?'

'No.'

'Sexy?

'No.'

'So it's all about money?'

'Agatha, you don't know what it means to have land. I'm damned if I'll part with an acre. I've worked and worked to make it pay. But I can probably kiss goodbye to the European Union farm subsidies. Besides, it's a business deal.'

'I don't get you.'

'I am being paid a big amount of money to marry her.'

'Why?'

'She's pregnant.'

'You shock me. You have to be paid to give your child your name?'

'Not my child. Some Spanish waiter called Angel. They met in Benidorm.'

'Benidorm! She can't be classy.'

'Common as muck. Father is a self-made man. Scrap yards all over the country and a chain of supermarkets.'

'Wouldn't this Angel be delighted to take the money instead of you?'

Charles sighed. 'He didn't stay around to hear

any offers. The minute he got a letter from her with the news, he disappeared. The restaurant is called A Little Bit of Blighty.'

'Look, Charles, don't do this. I'm a rich woman.'

'It's signed, sealed and delivered, Agatha. I am such a fool. I can't get out of it now. They'd take me to court. I'm off.'

I was sick of these murders anyway, thought Agatha defensively, as she hailed a taxi at Alicante Airport to take her to Benidorm. All she knew about Benidorm was that it was overcrowded with tourists and possibly one of the most unfashionable tourist spots in the world despite its popularity.

Her hotel was on the beach and called The Brit Experience. It turned out they were doing special rates for old-age pensioners and Agatha felt almost young as she passed through a foyer full of creaking oldies. The young man who carried her bags up to her room was slim, Spanish and attractive with a definite come hither gleam in his eye. Poor sod. Probably makes a bit on the side screwing the tourists, thought Agatha cynically.

She tipped him generously and asked, guessing he spoke perfect English, 'When is your evening off?'

'Why, this evening, madam. Would madam like a tour, a little dinner, a...'

'No. I am sure everyone in this dump speaks and understands English but I had better have an interpreter. What time?'

'Eighteen hundred hours.'

'Meaning six o'clock. I'll meet you downstairs,

we'll go for a drink and I'll tell you what I need. Here is a hundred euros in advance.'

He took the money, kissed her hand and gazed deep into her eyes.

'What is your name?' asked Agatha.

'Manuel.'

'I am not interested in sex, Manuel. I am a private detective.'

'Yes, madam.'

'You may call me Agatha.'

'Sure thing, babes.'

Agatha blinked but decided to let it go.

She was to find later that the fact she was a detective had prompted Manuel to use American cop show phrases.

When Manual joined her in the hotel foyer, an old lady with the largest false teeth Agatha had ever seen, shouted, 'Got yoursel' a good 'un there!' Her geriatric friends all cackled and grinned and nudged each other.

Agatha glanced sideways at Manuel's handsome face. Surely he couldn't service old ladies.

'Where is this place?' asked Agatha. 'Shouldn't we get a cab?'

'No, pardner. It's round the corner.'

A cold wind was blowing off the sea and Agatha was relieved when they turned into the shelter of a side street. 'Let's have a drink first,' said Agatha. 'In case you have to interpret, I'd better explain the situation.'

They stopped in a small bar-cum-café. Agatha ordered a gin and tonic and winced when she tasted it. It seemed to be one part tonic to three parts gin. Manuel ordered an espresso for himself. 'Drink affects the performance,' he said.

'The only performance you are going to perform for me is that of a translator,' said Agatha.

He grinned and shrugged and obviously did not believe a word of it.

Agatha told him what she wanted to do. He listened carefully. Then he said, 'I know this Angel. I am better looking, yes? So she marries me, yes?'

'No. With any luck she marries the father of her child.'

'Perhaps we cannot find him,' said Manuel sulkily.

'Then perhaps you will get no more money,' remarked Agatha, her bearlike eyes boring into him.

He raised his hands. 'Cool it. You're the boss, lady.'

A Little Bit of Blighty turned out to be a dark little bar draped in Union Jacks. 'Is this run by a Britisher?' asked Agatha.

'It was,' said Manuel, 'but they went broke so Angel's brother bought it cheap. Started doing the all-day breakfast with lot of chips and ketchup. Big earner. His name is Eduardo Perez.' He led the way into the bar where a hairy man in a tank top was polishing glasses.

Manuel began to speak in rapid Spanish. How sullen his face is, thought Agatha. When he brightens up I'll know when Manuel's got to the money bit. There we go. Expansive smile. Walk round the bar. Kiss my hand.

'Dear lady,' crooned Eduardo. 'Let's share a jug

178

of sangria. I have the best in Benidorm. You see, as it stood, Angel did not yet have the means to support a wife and child and, lady, I tell you from the heart, she swore she was on the pill. The father, he swore revenge so we decided to hide Angel. But if this Patreecia has found an English lord, why will she want my Angel?'

'He's not a lord. He's only Sir Somebody. Let Angel come to Britain with me. I will pay all expenses.'

'You wait here and tell you. You want the full English? On the house?'

'No, thank you.'

'OK. Manuel, pour the lady some sangria. I come back.'

Evidently Manuel could not believe that his sexual services were not going to be welcome that evening. He pressed Agatha's foot and then yelped when she kicked him in the shins.

'There's a table outside,' said Agatha. 'The smell of frying is choking me. Who is that poor woman I can see slaving in the kitchen?'

'She's British. Married to the previous owner. Sleeps with Eduardo when his wife won't. Cooks the breakfasts. See? Those two men are eating them.'

They found a table outside. The visitors here have either got tattoos, shaved heads or Zimmer frames, thought Agatha.

At last Eduardo returned followed by a man whom he introduced as Angel Perez. Agatha had expected someone like Manuel but Angel was in his forties, a small, wiry man with a figure like an acrobat. She demanded his identity papers and

179

then began to lay down the terms. Angel would come with her to England to meet Patricia. If it didn't work out, then Agatha would pay him five hundred euros and his airfares and expenses.

The brothers haggled for a long time until Agatha stood up and said impatiently, 'You are a waste of time.' They promptly accepted her terms. Agatha said she would collect Angel at lunchtime the following day and take him to the airport.

Outside the hotel, she paid Manuel another hundred euros and then had to stop him from following her up to her room. She sat on the edge of the bed and eased her feet out of a pair of high-heeled sandals. She began to wonder whether she had run mad. Charles was mercenary, Charles was a cheapskate. Why wasn't she letting him just get on with it?

Sir Charles Fraith sat alone in the library of his home with the door firmly locked. His fiancée and her parents were in residence. He had been frankly quite horrible to Patricia but she hardly seemed to notice, she was so taken up with being fitted for her wedding gown.

This evening was to be his engagement party. There was so much of her, he thought viciously. She had an arse as big as the Ritz and great big bosoms. She was five feet, ten inches in her stocking soles and tried to counteract it by stooping so she was round shouldered. Charles was drinking brandy to try to face up to the evening ahead. He knew if he broke off the engagement that Patricia's father would most certainly sue. He would get some top psychiatrist to say his daughter's self-esteem had been damaged. He had tried to phone Agatha, realising he had forgotten to invite her – or, said his conscience – deliberately forgotten to invite her. He wished she would arrive and bring that caustic view of things to maybe give him some courage. Agatha would surely point out that there was nothing up with the girl's appearance and he had no right to demand perfection in someone when he was so far from perfect himself.

Lulled by the brandy he had drunk, he fell into a deep sleep and only awakened when Gustav, his manservant, opened the library door with a spare key, woke Charles up and told him it was time to dress for the party.

'It is still possible to travel to France this evening.'

'I know. But I would be miserable everywhere with the thought of a lawsuit hanging over me.'

Gustav tenderly helped his master upstairs to his bedroom and then began to take out his evening clothes.

'You know, sir,' said Gustav, 'we should have thought of Agatha Raisin.'

'You can't stand her.'

'Now, the Hugginses over on the other side of Ardens Grafton hired a public relation's officer for help in promoting their estates. It was some years ago, but they are doing very well, practically outselling the Duchy of Cornwall when it comes to goods baked or made on the estate.'

'Why the hell didn't you tell me this before?'

'It was only brought to my mind owing to the present miserable circumstances.'

'Well, too late now. Nothing left to do but face

the firing squad. At least the announcement is first thing and then I can get really, truly drunk.'

When Charles mounted the steps to the platform at the end of the ballroom he wondered why it felt like mounting the steps of the scaffold. Patricia was waiting for him, dressed in white silk, draped and tucked and gored around her generous body. She had a great moonlike face and, to his irritation, she was chewing gum. He was seized by a great wave of physical revulsion. Her father, Sydney Brent-Arthurton, joined him on the platform. A sea of faces stared at them, Patricia's friends and family on one side and Charles's on the other. Down one side was a long buffet and bar.

Sydney lowered a microphone to his own mouth level and then signalled to the leader of the small band behind him. There was a drumroll.

'Folks,' began Sydney.

The double doors at the other end of the ballroom crashed open and a voice called, 'Patreecia. It's me. Your Angel.' Behind him stood Agatha Raisin.

Good heavens! She can look beautiful after all, thought Charles. For Patricia's face was lit up with love, *illuminated* with love as she held up her skirts and ran down from the platform, down the hall to throw herself into the Spanish waiter's arms.

Charles had only known Sydney as bullying and pompous but now he looked crushed. 'What do we do now?' he asked.

But the efficient Gustav was there to seize the microphone and announce, 'The buffet is open.

182

Please help yourselves.

'Perhaps we should all adjourn to the library?' suggested Gustav.

Agatha had fled. She felt she must have run mad. What girl was going to jilt Charles for a Spanish waiter? If Angel had looked like Manuel, it might have been possible.

Inside her cottage, she looked around for her cats and then remembered Doris had them. The loneliness seemed to press in on her. Outside, a November gale was blowing and leaves tapped at the windows and things skittered about in the thatch.

It was only nine o'clock in the evening but all she wanted to do was pull the duvet over her head and go to sleep.

She was just about to go up the stairs without supper although she was hungry when the doorbell rang. She had recently installed one of those video doorbells where you can see and speak to whoever is outside. Gustav was standing there.

'May as well get it over with,' muttered Agatha, opening the door.

Gustav followed her through to the kitchen, sat down on a chair and said solemnly, 'I must speak with you.'

'And here beginneth the first sermon,' snapped Agatha. 'Get on with it.'

'I have a proposition to put to you.'

'Out with it.'

'I do not want my master to make another unfortunate engagement. So he must make the place pay. You must tell him how to do it.'

183

'So he got out of the engagement?'

'Oh, that. Yes. Miss Patricia is in love with the Spaniard. Papa is going to buy them a restaurant in Benidorm. I managed to get the father to pay for the engagement party. Most difficult.'

'OK. That's a relief. So about this plan of yours, I know bugger all about crops and sheep and other beasties.'

Gustav's eyes, those black eyes that gave nothing away, fastened on her face. 'You could learn. How does Sir Charles get the public to pay for something?'

'You're a sort of butler, aren't you?' said Agatha. 'So buttle. Get me a coffee and a toasted cheese sandwich and maybe I might get an idea.'

Gustav took off his jacket and got to work. 'I am not a butler exactly,' he said over his shoulder as she switched on the coffee machine. 'I am a man of all trades. In other words, in these cheap days, I am several servants rolled into one.'

'You could earn a fortune in America.'

'I am allowed a lot of time off and Sir Charles bought me a Harley-Davidson which I love more than any woman, so why should I leave?'

He slid a mug of black coffee in front of Agatha followed by a toasted cheese sandwich.

'What made you think of me?' asked Agatha.

He told her of the landowners who had hired a public relations officer.

'Even if I pulled you out of the red, what's in it for me?'

'One per cent of all the takings for life.'

'That house of his is Victorian and ugly. What was there before it?'

'A Tudor building which belonged to Cater Thompson.'

'Who was he?'

'He was a member of the Hell Fire Club and held black masses and orgies.'

Agatha lit a cigarette. 'You wouldn't happen to have a portrait of him?'

'In the attics.'

'Look, Gustav, I know just how to get the ball rolling but you will get Charles to take me to a lawyer and I want the deal signed and delivered before I do any work.'

'Yes. But the idea must be the best.'

Agatha grinned. 'When it comes to PR, I am the best. Now shove off.'

Chapter Ten

But it turned out to be several weeks before Agatha met with Charles's lawyers to hammer out the deal. The agency became flooded with work and both Charles and the murders were forgotten. The cases were bread and butter, being the usual mix of divorces, lost pets, lost children, industrial espionage and shoplifting. Finally it was Patrick who saved the day by bringing in two moonlighting detectives who, having access to police files, cleared up a lot of cases for Agatha in record time. When she was finally able to relax, she phoned Gustav and asked him to set up a meeting. He promptly arranged it for three o'clock the following afternoon.

Agatha thanked the two detectives for all their good work and gave each of them a small bonus. Before they left, she asked them, 'Any tips to help me with those murders over at the witches' tree?'

The elder of the two scowled in deep thought. Then he said, 'There's always that one question you forgot to ask, that one question which could solve the whole case. Try to think of the question, Agatha.'

Agatha was beginning to feel annoyed with Charles as she set out to meet his lawyers at his home the next day. She felt she had already spent too much time and money on him. As she drove up the long drive to his ugly mansion, she couldn't help remembering how impressed she had been when she had first met him, how she had fretted over what to wear, terrified that some of her old Birmingham accent would poke up its common head through her carefully enunciated vowels.

When Gustav ushered her into the library and her eyes ranged from the two lawyers, or who she thought must be lawyers from their appearance, to the factor, James Blessop, whom she had met before, and then back to Gustav, she said, 'Where's Charles?'

'Sir Charles,' said Blessop, 'took off this morning, saying he had an awful hangover, and had to get away.'

'Then tell Sir Charles,' said Agatha, 'that he will receive a bill from me for a wasted morning getting out here and also for my Spanish expenses. The cheek of it!'

In vain did Gustav plead with her to wait while they tried to contact Charles. Agatha marched out and drove steadily to Oxford. Forget Charles. What question had she not asked? Well, she hadn't just asked Laura if she had killed her sister. Why not? Unless Laura had a tame assassin hidden in the back room, she was not strong enough to overpower her. Agatha brushed away a tear. She had hoped that a grateful Charles would have been there. Was that too much to ask?

But her innate sense of the ridiculous came to her rescue. Life was not like romances. Did she expect him to change because of the love of a good woman? And wasn't she, Agatha Raisin, what you would class as a good woman? She gave herself a mental shake. Forget Charles. Out there in the whole wide world was a man for her. Romance was not dead. It was hibernating. Like winter.

Feeling much more cheerful, she finally parked outside Laura's house and rang the doorbell. She waited and waited. An empty beer can rolled along the street chased by swirl of autumn leaves. Agatha recognised Laura's car. What if Laura was not a murderer but a murderee? What if she was lying mangled and dead on the floor?

Agatha tried the door handle. The door was locked. It had two stained-glass panes on the upper part. She went back to her car and took a tyre iron out of the boot, went back to the door and smashed one of the panes, put her hand gingerly through the broken glass and unlocked the door. She searched downstairs, in the living room, dining room, kitchen and office, before mounting the stairs. A bathroom, what looked like a guest bedroom and then another door. Agatha pushed it open and let out a gasp of dismay.

Laura was lying on her bed, fully dressed, her hands folded on her bosom. Her death mask of a face was clay white. Agatha stumbled down the stairs and once outside, phoned the police. Although it only took the police five minutes to arrive, it felt like half an hour to Agatha.

Two policemen listened as Agatha gabbled that Laura was dead. 'Wait there,' one of them ordered.

Agatha shivered, her arms wrapped round herself. Then to her horror, she heard a scream coming from upstairs in the house. One of the policemen came out, eyeing the broken pane of glass.

'Miss Darby is alive. She had a face mask on. She looked down at you from the window a minute ago. At first she referred to you as Madame Clouseau, but then said you were some sort of private detective called Agatha Raisin. She says she will not press charges but she will send you a bill for repairing the door and replacing the stained glass. Now I must ask you to accompany us to the station where we will take down your statement.'

By the time Agatha got back to Carsely, her rage against Charles had returned and burst out into open fury when she found him asleep on her sofa with the cats lying across him.

She went into the kitchen and collected a bottle of mineral water from the fridge, went back to the sitting room and poured the cold water over his face. He sat up spluttering while the cats fled.

He took out a handkerchief and fastidiously dried his face and mopped up water spilled on his clothes. 'Bitch,' he remarked.

'Selfish, self-centred bastard,' howled Agatha.

'Got something.' Charles fished down the side of the sofa and produced a magnum of champagne with a pink silk bow tied round the neck of the bottle. 'Deepest thanks, Aggie. Arranged with my accountant to pay your Spanish expenses so send him a bill and stop scowling at me and get out a couple of glasses.'

'Why weren't you at the meeting?'

'Went to buy this for you. Met an old school chum and got talking. Pour us some champers, Aggie.'

'Pour it yourself,' said Agatha. 'I'm weary and I'm in disgrace. I'll light the fire.'

The fire had been set by her cleaner so Agatha put a match to the kindling and sat back on her heels to watch the blaze. Then she moved to an armchair and kicked off her shoes.

Charles handed her a glass of champagne and sat on the floor at her feet. 'Out with it,' he said.

So Agatha told him how she had thought Laura was dead and Charles laughed and spluttered.

'I'm glad you find it funny,' she said.

'Well, it is. So PR of the ages, what's your big idea?'

'Got a damn good mind not to tell you,' mumbled Agatha.

'Have some more champagne and start the day all over again.'

'You've got Cater Thompson in your attic.'

'And you've got bats in yours. What are you talking about?'

'There was this Hell Fire Club member, Cater, who used to live in the old Tudor building and get up to all sorts of nasties. So you start by throwing a candlelit fundraiser for the Red Cross.'

'I do something for the Red Cross every year, so what's new?'

'The party's in the ballroom, is it?'

'Yes.'

'And you've got that pseudo-medieval minstrels gallery up above?'

'So?'

'There's a portrait of the old rip in the attics. You hang it prominently in the ballroom. Don't spend money on too many candles. Lots of shadows needed except from an electric light over Cater's portrait. Know any actresses?'

'I know Bethany Cross. She's sort of third maiden on the left at the Royal Shakespeare Company.'

'Anyway, someone like that. You get a hologram of Cater. She points up and shrieks. At first sight a transparent flickering impression. Get the press there. Make it wine and cheese. You wait until the fame of the ghost spreads out over the country-side and then you advertise tours of your house at ten pounds a head.

'Let me think,' Agatha went on. 'Before that actress sees the ghost, you get a fan set up some-where so that people can claim the room went suddenly cold. If it catches on, we get a gift shop with postcards of Cater and mugs and dishcloths. But I want four per cent, not one.'

'Greedy cow!'

'Cheapskate.'

'Your glass is empty, Aggie.'

'Tell me, Charles, what question haven't I asked?'

'Will you marry me?'

'Don't be frivolous. The murders. A detective said to me you had to think of that all-important question you should have asked.'

'I'll get a piece of paper and we'll start,' said Charles. 'Least I can do when you'll be slaving away for one per cent.'

'Four. And don't try to pull a fast one.'

'Right. Have paper, have pen. Let's start with Sir Edward.'

'Is he mad? What happened to you in the jungle?'

'Possible,' said Charles. 'Molly?'

Agatha took the bottle and helped herself to more champagne. 'What about this? Are you just a whore or do you murder people as well?'

'Too blunt,' said Charles.

'Laura Darby. Did you murder your sister?'

'I like that one,' commented Charles.

'Can't use it, she'll sue.'

'Garage chap. Margaret wasn't your type so it must have been the money. Were you so angry with her when she told you she wasn't leaving you any that you killed her?'

'I think,' said Agatha, 'that we are looking at this the wrong way. I think what that detective meant was: what question have you not asked yourself?'

'Let's sleep on it,' said Charles. 'If I slept with you, a bright idea might hit me.'

191

'What would hit you would be my fist,' said Agatha, fighting down a longing to be held.

Agatha awoke to the sound of the vacuum. She struggled awake, cursing that she had forgotten to set the alarm and then remembered it was Saturday, the day that Toni usually turned up to go over a few cases, but usually only for an hour. The vacuum was switched off and Agatha could hear Doris and Charles talking but couldn't make out the words. She got up, showered and dressed and went downstairs and then remembered she hadn't any make-up on.

Agatha fished what she called her emergency repair kit from a cupboard and started to make up her face. 'Bit unhygienic,' said Charles. 'A little cloud of blusher has floated into my croissant.'

'Then blow it off,' said Agatha. 'Got a croissant for me?'

'In the bag on the table.'

'Ta.'

'We could have some fun today,' said Charles.

'And I'm not up for it, sweetie.'

'Who's asking, you raddled old bag. Joke. Don't throw the coffee pot at me. I phoned Gustav last night about your idea and, as a start, he's bringing a magician over. I want to use the magician for something else. I want him to frighten the witches of Sumpton Harcourt into spilling what they know about the murders. Surely you want some revenge. Did they ever get charged for shoving a syringe in your neck?'

'No. No proof. Worth a try, this haunting idea.'

'He should be here soon.'

'Have you ever considered, Charles, that if you ever did get married that your wife might not like Gustav glooming around the place?'

The doorbell rang. Charles answered it and came back with only Gustav.

'Where's the magician?' asked Agatha.

'Jock's following on.'

'Jock doesn't sound very magician-like,' complained Agatha.

'He was billed as The Great Magico. Still is but he has to get gigs on the Continent, vaudeville having died,' said Gustav. 'Mrs Raisin, you have lipstick on your cheek.'

Agatha gave a squawk of dismay and decided to go upstairs and change her whole make-up. Who knows? This Jock might be attractive.

Once in her bedroom, she sat down at her dressing table mirror. It was an old Victorian one, Agatha having given up using the magnifying mirror in the bathroom. Too depressing and sort of self-punishing. She looked in the mirror and a white face, twisted and sneering, slowly smiled back at her.

Agatha screamed and screamed. Charles pounded up the stairs and opened the door and Agatha flew into his arms, babbling about the mirror. Putting her firmly aside, Charles looked in the mirror and saw nothing but his own face. The mirror was on top of a dresser. Charles suddenly leaned over the dresser and found himself looking into the ghastly face of a small man.

'Can I be of assistance?' came Gustav's voice.

'Get the police,' yelled Charles.

'That's Jock,' said Gustav. 'He wanted to show

Mrs Raisin just how good he could be.'

'You could have given me a heart attack,' screamed Agatha. 'Take your precious Jock and f–'

'Wait a bit, Aggie,' said Charles. 'If he frightened you, think of the effect on a pair of silly witches.'

Agatha stood with her head bowed.

'Can I come out now?' asked a plaintive voice from behind the dresser.

'Oh, come on,' said Agatha. 'But don't ever scare me again.'

Jock, when he emerged, turned out to be a small, very thin man. 'OK,' said Agatha, 'how did you do it?'

'Charles left the door open when he let Gustav in,' said Jock. 'I nipped up the stairs, saw the mirror, done that trick before, took the glass out, and Bob's your uncle.'

Agatha glared at Charles. 'All this get the police rubbish. You were in on this, Charles. All I want is to be free of this case and … and…' With that, Agatha burst into tears.

'You won't be free of it blubbing like a baby,' snapped Charles. 'Pull yourself together.'

Agatha socked him on the nose and he let out a yell of pain.

It was a sorry group who gathered in the kitchen. Gustav was serving out coffees laced with brandy. Agatha was sullen, Charles angry and nursing a sore nose and Jock was mentally doubling his fee.

As the brandy in the coffee began to warm her, Agatha reflected that if Jock's magic had caused *her* such an upset, what would it do to a couple of gullible witches?

'All right,' she said reluctantly. 'You're on. You will be paid a basic fee but only get a bonus if they're *really* scared.'

She opened up her laptop and showed Jock her notes on the mother and daughter who ran the café in Sumpton Harcourt. 'Their names are Josie and Tracy Fawkes, as in Guy. Previously charged for growing cannabis. Josie's mother was one of the coven ridiculed in the *Picture Post* all those years ago. There are three other witches that we know of in the coven because they were all arrested after I was attacked. When are you going to start work?'

'Right away. I need to case the café and living quarters.'

'Phil Marshal, one of my detectives, took a series of photographs,' said Agatha, bringing them up on her laptop.

After he had studied the photographs and made notes, Agatha made him sign a statement that he would only get a modest sum unless he was successful and then the amount would be generous and Charles witnessed it.

Jock went up to the bathroom to clean the greenish-white grease paint from his face that he had used in the haunting of Agatha.

Agatha began to pace up and down her kitchen. 'I hope he doesn't frighten one of them literally to death. Horrible pair but if they're innocent, I don't want a death on my conscience.'

Gustav covertly watched Agatha. He certainly did not want his boss to marry someone such as Agatha Raisin and had made sure it didn't happen in the past. But there was certainly something between the pair. They finished each other's sentences. Charles was looking over Agatha's shoulder at something on her computer and at one point he gave her a swift kiss on the cheek and Agatha smiled up at him.

'"*Sufficient unto the day is the evil thereof*",' said Gustav.

'Quite the little Jeeves, aren't you?' said Charles. 'Why are you quoting the Bible?'

'I was thinking of the witches,' said Gustav, who was actually thinking he would deal with a possible Charles-Agatha situation later.

'What's been bothering me is that stuff that knocked you out,' said Charles. 'What was it?'

'Some sort of date-rape drug. People used it to clean car tyres or something. I think it's been taken off the market.'

'GHB. It's one of the date-rape drugs. Can kill if too much is administered. So what's bothering me is this. I would have expected them to use one of their own plant drugs or bop you on the head. Margaret Darby was strangled and that policeman was hit on the head and smothered. I somehow can't see the witches being involved.'

'Well, I can,' said Agatha. 'You've changed your tune. This is all your idea.'

Josie and Tracy Fawkes brought down the steel shutters over the shop-cum-café front window and ran indoors, shivering. 'If anyone else talks about global warming. I'll put a curse on them,' said Tracy.

Her mother poured out two glasses of port.

'Bottoms up, lass. Should us have a go at that Raisin woman again?'

'Naw. Them police were something nasty. What's for dinner, ma?'

'Told you. Your wits are wandering. Nicked one o' the vicarage chickens. That daft Molly woman started trying to keep them. Nice bit o' roast chicken, although in my mind, it still do seem stupid calling 'em chickens when in my day they was hens and if fer cooking, you asked for a boiling fowl or roasting fowl.'

'Oh, yawn, ma. Who the hell cares what happened in your day. Who... What's that?'

'What's what?'

'Thought I heard something upstairs.'

'Tell you what, my lass. Let's go to the pub for one afore supper. Jem Thatchell's keen on you and he's got a tidy farm. Put a bit o' make-up on.'

'Right, ma.'

Tracy went up to her bedroom under the thatched eaves. She sat down at her dressing table and took out her box of cosmetics. Her mirror had two sides: one magnified, the other plain. Tracy didn't feel like facing her magnified image and so she twisted the mirror round to the ordinary side. She searched her make-up collection for her precious bottle of Dior foundation cream which she had stolen from Harvey's in Mircester. She got up and opened her bedroom door. 'Ma!' she yelled. 'You bin pinching my make-up?'

'Wouldn't be seen dead in it,' came her mother's reply.

Tracy turned to go back to her seat when she

saw that bottle of Dior. It appeared to have rolled into a far corner of the room. Clucking impatiently, she picked it up and returned to the dressing table.

She unscrewed the top of the bottle, put a little on one hand and leaned forward to study her reflection. A neighbour was to say that the wail Tracy let out was like the wail of one of those American trains you saw on television, racing through the Midwest.

For to Tracy, that face looked like a demon from hell with glaring red eyes. Her mother came pounding up the stairs. It took quite a time for Mrs Fawkes to calm her shaking, incoherent daughter down. But when she heard what had happened, she walked to the mirror and whispered, 'Is that you, my lord?' But only her own reflection stared back at her.

'There's nothing there,' she grumbled. 'You bin seeing things.'

'Oh, ma. I'm frit. Do you think the master is punishing us? We should never ha' called on him.'

'We'll call on him tomorrow as usual. You'll see. It'll be all right, lass. Come on. Forget the pub. Chicken looks great.'

But when they returned to the kitchen, it was to find that the chicken had gone.

'You silly cow!' raged Mrs Fawkes. 'Devils be damned. That was someone playing tricks on you, Trace-girl, in order to get their hands on my... Check the money. Quick!'

Tracy went to a low cupboard in the corner of the kitchen and brought out a large, white, enamel tin bearing the legend FLOUR. She opened it and fell back with a great scream. For a jack-in-the box had sprung up and now hung over the edge of the tin. Of the money, they discovered, there was no sign.

Agatha and Charles waited for Jock to return to see if he had scared some sort of confession out of them.

'After Jock left, you were away for some time,' said Charles suspiciously. 'Where did you go?'

'Well, if you must know, I wanted to be sure Jock was playing fair. I tell you, Charles, I feel sure that one has done time in prison. Phil said in his report that they spent all their free time in their kitchen. I stuck a powerful tape recorder on their kitchen window just below the extractor fan. I told Simon to go and pick it up while you were in the bathroom.'

The doorbell rang. 'That's either Jock or Simon.' Charles went to answer it and came back with Simon.

He handed Agatha her tape recorder. 'Listen to it?' asked Agatha.

'Haven't had time,' said Simon.

Agatha switched it on. They heard shrieks and yells coming from the kitchen as the missing chicken was discovered along with their money. And then Josie Fawkes's terrified voice. 'It's the Master,' she said in an anguished voice. 'We done displeased him, that's what. We was ever so careful. Told that daft bitch, Darby, there was a handsome man waiting for her in the woods by the praying rock like he asked.'

'What'll we do?' wailed Tracy. 'We didn't tell

199

the others in the coven. He says as how we were special.'

'We'll go up to the prayer rock tonight at midnight and call on him,' said Josie. 'He'll know what to do.'

Then a scream and cries of, 'Who the hell are you?'

'Evening, ladies,' came Jock's voice. 'Now that was an interesting conversation you just had. So you helped our murderer. The police would be interested, but if you report the loss of your money, then I will tell them what I heard. It's no use creeping behind me with that rolling pin, Mrs Fawkes. I have a gun and I can easily shoot you both dead. Now good evening to you both. It's been fun. Only a pair of silly bitches like you would go on about this Master. You've helped a very human murderer.'

There came a scraping sound as Simon detached the tape recorder.

'Gustav,' said Charles. 'Where did you find this magician?'

'I employed him at the last fête,' said Gustav defensively. 'He told fortunes. Great success.'

'And do you think he'll turn up here?'

'Bound to,' said Gustav. 'He'll want his money.'

'I'm not waiting,' said Agatha. 'I'm going to that rock at midnight to see who this Master is.'

Charles stifled a yawn. 'Do it the easy way, Agatha. Phone the police.'

'No! Why should I do all the groundwork and let them take the praise? Gustav, you wait here and see if he has the nerve to turn up. Where is this prayer rock anyway?'

'Everything's on the internet now,' said Simon. 'I'll look it up.'

He fiddled about on his iPad and then said, 'Got it! It was used by Protestants for services during the reign of Bloody Mary.'

'And how do we get there?' asked Agatha.

'There's a map here. A mile outside the village to the north, along a footpath through the woods and it is only a few yards off the road.'

'Right. I'm going to put flat shoes and trousers on,' said Agatha. 'Master, indeed!'

'Could be Mistress,' said Charles. 'You know, a woman masquerading as a man.'

'We'll see.'

But it was just after midnight when they reached the rock because Charles had said as he had a big car they should use his and had run out of petrol. So Simon had to walk back to Agatha's where he had left his motorbike, get a spare can of petrol from the shed at the bottom of Agatha's garden and ride back with it. Agatha had shouted at Charles and called him a cheapskate, so when Simon returned it transpired that Charles had simply got out of the car and walked away.

So Agatha and Simon located the footpath and made their way to the rock. There was no sign of Josie and Tracy. 'It's thanks to bloody Charles putting half a cup of petrol in his tank that we've lost a chance to maybe find the murderer,' grumbled Agatha.

The footpath turned sharply and a wedge-shaped rock rose up black against a moonlit sky.

Behind Agatha whispered Charles's voice,

'There's something on the rock.'

Stifling a scream, Agatha swung round. 'Where the hell have you been?' she hissed.

'Oh, do shut up! I don't work for you, you tiresome, bad-tempered bitch. Are you going up there to see what's on top of the rock or do I have to do it?'

'I'll go,' said Simon.

They waited impatiently. 'Are you sure you saw something on the rock?' demanded Agatha.

'Looked like black on blackness,' said Charles. 'Just an impression.'

Simon came back. 'It's Jock. He's dead. It's awful.'

'How did he die?'

'I don't know,' wailed Simon. 'His head's covered in blood. Get the police.'

'Wait a minute. We'd better get our stories straight,' said Agatha. 'We'll have to admit that Jock or whatever his name is is a magician we hired to entertain people at Charles's home. Nothing about playing a ghost. We don't want to ruin that idea before it's off the ground. But we'll say we were talking about the case while we were engaging him.'

'So what are we doing here?' asked Simon.

'Let me think. I know. I sent you to detect. You were asking about the witches and were told that Josie and her daughter often went to the praying rock. You told me and I came running.'

'I'd better phone my lawyer,' said Charles. 'Wilkes is going to have a field day. I can hear him now. "How does it come about, Sir Charles, that you just happen to be at the prayer rock and just *happen* to find the dead man, who, by some amazing coincidence, is a magician you were about to hire for a fête?"'

'Wait a bit,' said Agatha. 'We could save ourselves a lot of trouble if we just cleared off and made sure we didn't leave a trace. Anonymous phone call.'

'Sounds great to me,' said Charles. 'Anyone got a torch?'

'I have,' said Simon.

'Shine it along the path and wipe out any footprints as we leave,' said Charles. 'You didn't leave your fingerprints anywhere, Simon?'

'No, I wore gloves.'

'We'll call in at the vicarage,' said Charles. 'Gives us an excuse for being in the village.'

'After midnight? Forget it,' said Agatha. 'Oh, how frustrating this all is! Somehow we've got to find the identity of this Master, for Josie and Tracy don't seem to know. Simon, before you roar off on your bike, phone from a box in Mircester. Oh, and make sure when I pull out I haven't left any tracks or, if I have, get rid of them.'

'It is *my* car and my driver's seat, Aggie,' said Charles, 'so get out of the driver's seat both literally and metaphorically.'

They drove home to find a note from Gustav on the kitchen table saying that Jock hadn't turned up. He had also left Jock's name and address and telephone number.

'I'm off,' said Charles. 'What a night!'

'Charles. Could you stay?'

'Beg.'

'I'm begging.'

'All right. One goodnight kiss and… What's up? You look as if you've just been struck by lightning.'

'I've remembered the one question I should have asked!'

Chapter Eleven

'What question?' asked Charles. 'What are you talking about?'

Agatha hurriedly reminded him about that detective saying there was always one question you forgot to ask.

'So what is the question?'

'Who inherits?'

'Your wits are wandering. The Dogs Trust inherits. Before that Laura, before her Guy.'

'But who came before Guy?'

'I don't get it.'

'Listen! I feel money is the cause of the murder. I think the whole attraction Margaret Darby had was her money and I think she knew it and used it. Guy was right about Molly as it turns out; John Hardcotte really did believe Laura's malice. There's an unknown somewhere. I'll phone Patrick.'

'It's the middle of the night!'

'I can't wait.' Agatha dialled Patrick's number. When the detective answered, Agatha could hear the sound of clinking glasses and boozy voices in the background.

'Are you in a lockdown?' asked Agatha, meaning a pub that allowed the favoured few to drink on into the small hours.

'No, it's a wake for an old friend of mine. Killed on duty.'

'Shot?'

'Overactive girlfriend wore him out. Died on the job.'

'Patrick, you wouldn't happen to know if anyone was due to inherit Margaret Darby's money before, say, Guy Harris?'

'Can you wait till I dig up my notes on my phone? I'll call you back.'

'I would like to go to bed,' pleaded Charles.

'Don't you want to hear what he says?'

'No. And I think you should get some sleep as well.'

But Agatha's eyes were glittering. 'I feel it's the answer. Oh, stop yawning in my face and go to bed.'

Charles ambled off. Agatha waited and waited. Finally her phone rang. At first she could barely hear Patrick because of male voices roaring out some filthy song until he shouted he would take his phone outside.

While she waited, Agatha felt suddenly flat. What had seemed like a great leap of intuition now seemed like grasping at straws.

Patrick's voice came back on the phone. 'Right, let's see. The damn woman changed her will as often as her knickers. The one before Guy? Someone called Benjamin Gentry.'

Bengy, by all that's holy, thought Agatha. Let's think this through. Neither Bengy nor his sister works for a living. Probably money from one of those family trusts. Money stays the same over the years but the economy doesn't and so a life of luxury becomes a good middle-class income and then austerity. She suddenly realised Patrick was saying plaintively, 'I'd like to go back to the party.'

'Oh, sure, go ahead.'

Agatha ran up the stairs and into the spare room where Charles was now lying asleep. 'Wake up!' shouted Agatha, jumping on the bed.

Charles woke up and grabbed hold of her, rolled her on her back and began to kiss her. And somehow, it was only the following morning when Agatha woke up and noticed her clothes had been thrown around the spare room and that Charles had gone that she remembered she hadn't told him about Bengy.

But when she had showered and dressed and rushed downstairs, it was to find he had really gone. He had not even left a note. To Agatha, it was all like a slap in the face. It seemed as if Charles had helped himself to her body in the same way as he helped himself to her cigarettes. She put on her coat and went off to the comfort of Mrs Bloxby.

She had only been gone ten minutes when Charles came back carrying a bouquet of flowers and a bag of fresh croissants. He ran upstairs to wake Agatha and found that she had gone. He felt just as if she had slapped him in the face. So he went home and gave the flowers to his aunt and moodily ate the croissants himself.

The vicar told Agatha sharply that his wife was

not at home. He then retreated to his study where his wife found him a few moments later. 'Who was at the door, dear?'

'Jehovah's,' said the vicar.

He didn't like lying to his wife but he felt Agatha was a bad influence. He thought she had few morals and might corrupt his wife.

Agatha walked back through the steel grey morning, feeling suddenly afraid. The police would question everyone in the village and get to Josie and Tracy who might say they had been robbed. Maybe the police would start asking Jock's girlfriends or relatives and one of them might say that Jock had talked about being paid to frighten Josie and her daughter. Some weirdo playing at being the devil was bumping off people like a psychopath. Maybe he would come after her next. Then Charles would be sorry! Damn Charles. No, he wasn't going to get away with it. She had a right to demand an explanation. So she got into her car and drove out to his mansion. As she motored up the long drive, a voice on the radio was talking about global warming as one small pellet of snow bounced off the windscreen to be followed by another and another.

By the time she hammered on the front door, the snow was blowing in white sheets.

Gustav answered the door and barred her way. 'We are not at home,' he said.

Agatha gave him an enormous push. 'Oh, yes, we are,' she snarled. 'How dare you try to leave me out in a blizzard.'

The library door opened and Charles said in a

cold voice, 'What the hell do you want?'

'It's private.'

'Like hell.'

'OK, if you want Gustav to hear the intimate details of last night, I'll begin.'

'Oh, shut up. Come into the library.'

Agatha followed him in and then turned and slammed the door. 'You bed me for the night and clear off in the morning without even leaving a note as if I were some tart you'd rented for the night. Stop laughing. It's not funny.'

'Listen, Aggie. I came back bearing flowers and croissants and I thought you had cleared off, casting me off like a worn-out glove as my great-granny would have put it.'

'I'm sorry,' said Agatha in a small voice. 'I'm so hungry. I'd love a croissant.'

'Well, I'm sorry. Because I ate them all and gave the flowers to my aunt. I'll take you out for a full English at the nearest greasy spoon.'

'Lovely thought,' said Agatha. 'But it's snowing a blizzard.'

'Sun's shining,' said Charles, looking out of the window. 'Nothing more than a shower.'

An hour later, after a plate of ham, sausage, eggs, black pudding, mushrooms, tomatoes, beans and chips and two slices of toast, Agatha felt her waistband was about to cut off her circulation.

'You've got a business to run,' said Charles.

'Oh, Toni goes ahead and runs it. I'm often tempted to turn the whole thing over to the girl and be a lady of leisure. No more murders. No more frights.'

208

'I think you'd better solve this one or the killer may come after you. What can we do about Bengy? Accuse him?'

'That might be an idea,' said Agatha slowly. 'He'd come after me. But if I had you and all my detectives, then I'd be safe and we'd get him.'

'I'll come with you to the office and see what they all think.'

It's never like books or the movies, thought Agatha later. Charles was supposed to say, 'No, my precious, you must not put yourself at risk.' Nor had he said one word of love. And he had eaten all those croissants like the pig he was. Agatha looked across her office at him as he lay lounging on the sofa, barbered, impeccable and impregnable.

Simon finally came in. 'So now that you are all here,' began Agatha. 'I want you all to hear my plan to catch the murderer.' She went on to say that she would visit Bengy that very evening and they were all to lurk outside. She had collected a doorbell from the hardware. If she was in danger, she would press the doorbell, the receiver would be outside with the watchers and would emit a huge sound like a New York police car.

'Can't you just go to the police?' asked Simon.

'And say what?' demanded Agatha. 'They'd just laugh at me. No proof.'

'Don't drink anything,' warned Toni. 'All he needs to do is drug your drink. We won't hear anything suspicious and, by the time we've decided to investigate, he'll have cleared off.'

Patrick looked at Agatha speculatively. All she

was suggesting offended his ex-cop soul. And yet none of them had the resources of the police. He gave a slow nod. 'I can give you a Mace spray.'

Agatha had a moment of weakness. Surely someone, anyone, would volunteer to go in her place. At last, she gave a little sigh and said, 'Let's get it over with. If I wait until tomorrow, I'll lose courage.'

Agatha was wired up by Patrick, who was explaining he would be listening in a van he had borrowed from some police station – 'Don't ask' – and assured Agatha that at the first sign of trouble, they would rush into the place.

Toni had been told of the plan but she did not like it one bit. Someone had already shoved a syringe of date-rape drug into her neck. What was to stop them doing it again? By the time they all crashed into the place it might be too late. She got out of her car and crept round the back of the house. The moon above was bright and showed there were gnomes in the back garden as well. They had little labels on each. Toni took out a pencil torch and read some of the labels. They were all puns: gnome from gnome; honey, I'm gnome; gnome is where the heart is; and so on. Toni began to be even more worried. Surely there must be a streak of madness in the Gentrys. She moved quietly up to the kitchen door and took out the latest in electronic lock picks, highly illegal and bought on a visit to Germany. She quietly opened the kitchen door and crept in.

On the other side of the house, Bengy was welcoming Agatha. 'Our favourite detective,' he cried. 'I owe you dinner. So shaming to be caught out like that. Come in!'

He stood aside and Agatha walked past him into a tiny hall. 'Door on your left,' he called. Brenda Gentry rose to her feet. 'Hello, detective,' she said. 'Take a pew.'

Now, in most households, 'take a pew' is just a jokey way of saying, 'have a seat'. But in this mad household, there were two church pews on either side of the fireplace. Agatha looked around. There was a round table by the window with four upright chairs. 'I'll take one of those,' she said. 'Got a bad back.' She noticed that the window was stained glass, depicting some saint being pierced with spears.

'I see you're admiring our window,' said Bengy's voice behind her, making her jump. 'Brenda and I found them demolishing some old church the other side of Mircester and rescued the pews and that window. Like a gin? That's your tipple, isn't it?'

'I'm driving. No, thanks.'

'Coffee?'

'No, I've got something to say to you.'

'Wait till we sit down. Legs ain't what they used to be.'

Brother and sister pulled out a couple of hard chairs and sat on either side of Agatha.

This is ridiculous, thought Agatha. We're sitting in a row. Oh, get it over with.

She tried to speak but nerves seemed to have choked her voice. 'Sorry,' she said. 'Frog in my throat.'

'As the Princess said when the frog French

211

kissed her,' said Bengy and his sister gave a great bellow of laughter.

'I think you murdered Margaret Darby,' said Agatha, her own voice sounding unnaturally loud in her ears.

'You are doing it the wrong way,' said Bengy amiably. 'You are supposed to have a room full of people and go from one to the other, accusing each, until – aha! – you're the one, matey, or whatever Poirot would say. I'm curious. Why would I kill the old trout?'

'Because she promised to leave you everything in her will,' said Agatha. 'Then she changed her mind. Everyone seemed to want Margaret's money and she played on that.'

'This is where I should do the outraged bit,' said Bengy. 'How dare you come into my home and all that sort of stuff. I mean, what proof do you have?'

Agatha had a sudden flash of brilliance. 'Oh, don't be deceived. Josie and Tracy know the identity of the Master. The police are on their way but I want you to tell me why you did it.'

Out in the car, Patrick crossed his fingers.

'Well, let's say I did do it. Brenda, darling, get me a Scotch. Ever so thirsty. Margaret started sniffing around and promising the money if I would only deflower her. She read romances, you know. So comes the big night. Do you know, I couldn't get it up. Maybe it was her false teeth grinning at me from a jar by the bed.'

'And that made you kill her?'

'Oh, no! She came back with a hammer that same night and she killed Cuthbert and Jeremy.'

'Who?'

'Our very best gnomes. So she had to go. Right, Brenda, darling?'

'Right!'

It happened so quickly that Agatha was taken completely by surprise. Brenda whipped a belt round Agatha, pinning her to her chair, and, as she opened her mouth to scream, Bengy shoved a handkerchief in it soaked in GHB. Agatha passed out almost immediately.

'What'll we do with her?' horrified Patrick and Charles heard Bengy say. They were parked some way away, not wanting to be noticed.

Toni opened the door a crack and then switched on a powerful recording.

Bengy and Brenda stood transfixed as a great voice roared, 'Come out with your hands up. You are surrounded.'

'What are we going to do?' wailed Brenda.

'We'll bluff our way out of this. They won't have any forensic proof and who on earth is going to believe Josie and Tracy?'

Patrick at first could not believe how calm and accommodating the pair were as they came out with their hands up and meekly allowed him to handcuff them. While they waited for the police to arrive, Rory came over from the vicarage and Simon suggested that, instead of waiting for the ambulance, perhaps Rory might rush Agatha to hospital.

Then Brenda began to cry and said she had to go to the toilet. Toni came out of the house holding up a forensic bag through which the syringe could be seen clearly.

'Won't work, Brenda,' said Toni. 'I've got it.'

Brenda began to cry in earnest.

The police arrived, squads of them, headed by Wilkes. To Toni's relief, the ambulance arrived just as Rory and Simon were carrying Agatha from the house. To Toni's fury, she was not allowed to go with Agatha, and neither was Charles. They were to stay and give their statements. Charles saw Bengy's white face at the police car window and picked up the nearest gnome and hurled it against the house. His last sight of Bengy Gentry was that of a face contorted with grief.

In some parts of the police force, snobbery exists, and so when Bengy hired the services of a top criminal barrister, he was treated carefully and not watched as assiduously as he should have been. He hanged himself in his cell. Brenda, on hearing the news, died of a massive stroke. Bengy had not confessed to anything during the police interview but Brenda had, and Josie and Tracy were arrested as aiding and abetting a murderer. Their pleas that they thought it was the devil who was commanding them did not stop them being locked up for a year in a remand prison.

Epilogue

Agatha took a long time to recover. At first they thought her brain might have been affected because she barely spoke. It was only when Toni sneaked her two cats in and let them out on her bed that Agatha petted them and fussed and her face slowly came to life.

As the days of recovery passed into weeks and spring returned to the Cotswolds, Agatha found she could not bear the idea of going back to work. In her little front garden, the lilac tree which gave its name to the lane was bent down under a heavy load of blossom. James's cottage had been repaired but he was rumoured to be still travelling abroad.

One sunny day, Agatha was lying in a lounge chair in her garden when Charles breezed in. 'It's alive! It's alive!' he cried. 'I thought you had turned into a zombie. I called at the office but was told you were still convalescent. Why aren't you at work?'

'I'm thinking of not going back,' said Agatha.

'Why?'

'My spirit is broken.'

'You sound like a trashy novel. Fortunately Jock has disappeared and the horrible Fawkeses are not going to talk about any missing money as they ought to have been paying the taxman. Anyway, they're in the cooler. The reason I have called is that this afternoon sees the birth of my ghost. You've got to come along. Didn't Gustav call?'

'Yes, he came chattering about how he wanted me to call the media and I told him to get lost and do it himself. I gave him a list of contacts.'

'You've got to come because, if it isn't a success, you've got to tell us what we got wrong. And put some damn make-up on. I feel I've lost you. I want the old Agatha back.'

Agatha went upstairs and looked in the mirror. Her face had a tired, lost look. She was wearing a washed-out housedress and flat sandals. Her legs were hairy.

She shaved her legs and put on a short skirt over black tights and comfortable knickers. Then a white cotton blouse. Next came the high-heeled sandals. She winced, wondering how on earth she had managed to wear heels like this, day in, day out.

She applied make-up, including bright pink lipstick, and gave her reflection a reluctant smile. 'Welcome back, Agatha,' she said, and went down to join Charles.

When Agatha arrived at Charles's mansion an hour before the doors were due to open, she went from room to room and then demanded more candles. 'You've made it too gloomy. They'll be wandering off or bumping into the furniture. Where is the bar for the press?'

'Didn't think we needed one. We're supposed to be making money, not giving it away.'

'A liquored press is a happy press; a grumpy,

thirsty press is highly dangerous.'

'Oh, all right. Gustav, set it up in the morning room.'

I wonder why I used to be so keen on PR, thought Agatha, as the doors were finally opened.

Her feet ached and she wandered off through the cool rooms to find a quiet corner in which to sit down. She decided to try the library. It was Charles's favourite room and he would not let any of the day's visitors near it. She sank down into an armchair. Charles! He had done it again. He had made love to her and yet he had said not one word of love. Why did they call it making love? Rutting would be a better description, she thought sourly. The windows were open, letting in a fresh breeze.

Agatha eased off her sandals and wiggled her toes. She was just drifting off to sleep when she heard a whispering, whistling sort of chant from somewhere behind her, saying something like, 'Doom to you, Agatha. Doom and the wrath of hell.' And then some incomprehensible mutterings.

'Oh, fun's over.' With a groan, she bent down and put her sandals on again. 'Charles,' said Agatha, 'I'm tired and I'm going home.'

She stood up and let out a gasp. Josie and Tracy, in long black robes decorated with suns, moons and stars and their faces painted green, were leering at her.

'Well, well,' said Agatha. 'Who let the dogs out?'

'We're gonna kill yer,' moaned Tracy. 'We're gonna call on the Master.'

217

'Your Master turned out to be Benjamin Gentry who hanged himself in his cell.'

''Tis Satan himself we done a-calling,' crooned Josie.

They were between Agatha and the door. She saw an old-fashioned bell rope by the fireplace and wondered if it worked. But even if it did, there would be no one in the servants' hall to hear it. Or there might be some sort of cook-house-keeper. She gave the bell rope a hearty tug.

In the kitchen, Mrs Jordan, cook and housekeeper, was enjoying a bottle of beer while entertaining her daughter, Bella.

The bell jangled on its wire and Mrs Jordan stared in amazement. 'Well, I'll be damned. That's Sir Charles. Bound to be. He's got a damn cheek. They goes on as if we're in the Dark Ages. I tell you, I'm going up there to give him a piece of my mind. He's got that Gustav creature to fetch and carry for him.'

Agatha was beginning to become frightened. Josie had produced a wicked-looking knife from her robes and was carving signs in the air.

The door suddenly crashed open and the thin, wiry figure of Mrs Jordan stood there. She stared at Josie open-mouthed and then began to laugh. 'Oh, you're part of the act,' she said, and before Agatha could stop her, she went back out and slammed the door. But Mrs Jordan's arrival had managed to distract Josie and Tracy. Agatha dived through the open window, kicked off her sandals and ran as fast as she could until she saw a gardener and shouted at him to call the police.

It was all better than Charles had hoped. He had expected only the local papers to write about the ghost, but the nationals came out with the attempted attack on Agatha. The Fawkes' trial had been brought forward and a well-meaning but naïve psychiatrist had pleaded that Josie and Tracy had been led astray and so they had got off with only light sentences of community service.

When all the police questioning and questions from the press and television were over, Agatha and Charles retreated to her cottage.

'Let's get the six o'clock news,' said Charles, turning on the television.

There was only a brief report on the national news. 'Local news coming up next,' said Agatha. 'Bound to be something there. I hope this hasn't taken away any chance of publicity for our house, Charles. Oh, damn. It's all about Josie and Tracy.'

'Look, here's Gustav,' cried Charles.

He was introduced as Sir Charles's butler and then asked for his views on the attempt on Agatha.

'Oh, that lady is always getting attacked,' said Gustav dismissively.

'Bastard!' howled Agatha.

'But this house is cursed,' said Gustav. 'I'm telling you, and the visitors behind me will bear me out, the very ghost of Cater Thomson appeared this afternoon. The legend is that should he appear, murder will be done.'

He went on to describe the wicked life of Cater in a deep and gloomy voice worthy of Lurch in

219

The Addams Family.

'He ought to be on the stage,' said Agatha. 'Well, after his performance, you can start to charge visitors. You'll be coining it.'

'And so will you,' said Charles. '"Agatha Raisin Solves Another Case that Has Baffled the Police."'

'And I swear that the police are welcome to any future murders,' said Agatha. 'I am turning the agency over to Toni.'

'My dear girl, you'll die of boredom! What on earth will you do?'

'Maybe I'll get married.'

'Who is this fellow you've been keeping a secret?'

'His name is Arthur Allen and he's a banker. My age, but very fit.'

'So why have I never met this suitor?'

'I've been making sure you didn't. You've spoiled romances for me in the past.'

'Usually just before the fellow succeeded in murdering you. What's up with this one?'

'Nothing at all.'

'Married before?'

'No.'

'Aggie! If the chap's fit and healthy and your age and hasn't been married before, he's gay.'

'Anything but.'

'I'm off,' said Charles abruptly. 'Don't get up.'

Agatha wandered into the garden followed by her cats. She slumped down on a lounge chair. It was a pity, she reflected, that Arthur was only a figment of her imagination. Charles was supposed to say, 'Marry me!' I hate Charles, she thought fiercely.

The cordless phone on the garden table in front of her rang shrilly. It was Mrs Bloxby. 'I am actually giving a little dinner party tonight to welcome a newcomer to the village,' she said. 'He might get a chilly welcome because of his job.'

'What's that? Reporter? Politician?'

'No, he's a banker with Midland and West. Do say you'll come.'

'All right. What's his name?'

'Mr Arthur Andrews.'

Agatha laughed. 'You couldn't make him a Mr Allen, could you?'

'Why?'

'I'll tell you later. What time?'

'Come for drinks at seven.'

Agatha had told Toni of her plans to turn the running of the agency over to her, and, as it was, she only spent one or two days a week at work. As she dressed carefully for Mrs Bloxby's dinner party, she felt a pleasurable feeling of anticipation. What would this Arthur be like? She put on a long, scarlet, silk evening coat embroidered with golden dragons, wondering if it was too much, and then deciding it was all right. Under it she wore a simple black silk chiffon dress. Sheer black stockings and high-heeled shoes completed the ensemble. Carefully applied make-up and a spray of Givenchy's Hot Couture and Agatha felt she was looking her best.

Because of her very high heels, she drove the short distance to the vicarage, not wanting to risk breaking a heel on the cobbled streets. The spring air held a touch of warmth. Forsythia gleamed golden in gardens already shining with a bright show of daffodils.

Agatha experienced a rare feeling of peace. No more murders. As she got out of the car, a blackbird sang from the vicarage rooftop, and Agatha stood transfixed by the beauty of the sound.

As she entered the vicarage and was led into the drawing room by Mrs Bloxby, Agatha surveyed the guests and muttered, 'Well, from the sublime to the gor-blimey.'

For one of the men rising to meet her was new to her and must be the banker. He was small and squat with a blue chin and thick black eyebrows. 'May I introduce Mr Halburton,' said Mrs Bloxby.

Agatha heaved a sigh of relief. 'Where is your newcomer?'

'Not here yet. The rest I think you know.' Two sets of husbands and wives.

The doorbell rang again. Agatha sat down and crossed her long legs in their sheer black stockings and let her evening coat fall open.

Charles walked in. He raised his eyebrows at the look of disappointment on Agatha's face. He had been sure on reflection that she had made this banker up. As Charles went round shaking hands with the other guests, the doorbell rang again.

Mrs Bloxby led a middle-aged man into the room. He had a pleasant square face and thick grey hair.

Before Mrs Bloxby could introduce him, Agatha said, 'Just make it first names. So difficult anyway trying to remember who's who.'

So Charles only heard 'Arthur'. Agatha was

seated next to the banker at the dinner table and heaved a sigh of relief.

Mrs Bloxby announced that dinner was ready now that everyone was present. Agatha suddenly wondered where the vicar was. But, she thought, as she found to her relief that she was to sit next to Arthur and that Charles was at the other end of the table, it was just as well because Alf the vicar did not like her and might have been a drawback to her trying to charm this banker.

Agatha fidgeted while Arthur talked to a Mrs Dawson on his other side. A crumpled old gentleman like a tortoise was on the other side. Agatha tried to engage him in conversation, but he was very deaf.

At last, she heard Arthur addressing her. 'So I get to meet the famous detective,' he said.

'And I get to meet a handsome banker,' said Agatha, fluttering her long eyelashes at him. But the eyelashes were false and Agatha could sense that the right one was coming loose. She muttered a hurried excuse and fled the room, not to the bathroom but to the kitchen where Mrs Bloxby was just taking the roast out of the oven.

'Glue,' panted Agatha, 'quick.' Mrs Bloxby slid open a drawer and handed Agatha the tube. Agatha retreated to the bathroom and put a dab of the stuff to moor the sliding false eyelash in place. It was only then she noticed the glue was a kind that was super adhesive and supposed to be able to lift iron bars. She wondered frantically if she would have to report to the hospital later to get one eyelash removed.

She returned to the table. Charles was carving

a large leg of lamb, deftly putting slices on plates and passing them down the table.

'Are you all right?' Agatha realised Arthur was asking. 'Your right eye is all red.'

Agatha decided that charming Arthur and trying to make Charles jealous were not worth losing the sight of an eye, so she told him what had happened.

'Do you think Mrs Bloxby has nail varnish remover?' he asked.

'Unlikely,' said Agatha.

But Arthur got up and bent over Mrs Bloxby and whispered. Mrs Bloxby nodded and left the room, returning with a bottle of nail varnish remover. Arthur pocketed it, went back to Agatha and said, 'Let's go to the bathroom. I'll have you right in no time at all.'

Charles watched them exit. He raised his voice. 'What's up with Aggie?' he asked.

'Mrs Raisin has something in her eye. Please pass the mint sauce, Sir Charles.'

Charles half-rose to his feet but Mrs Bloxby said severely, 'I would like another slice of lamb.'

In the bathroom, Agatha, free of her false eyelashes and free of the glue, smiled at Arthur and joked, 'My hero.'

'Glad to help a little lady.' He grabbed hold of her and deposited a wet kiss on her mouth and shoved a great fat tongue between her lips while lifting her skirt.

Agatha shoved his head away, slapped down his hand and said, 'What the hell do you think you are doing?'

'Not my fault,' said Arthur sulkily. 'Went for a tour of that haunted house out in Warwickshire. Chap there told me you were hot stuff and liked a bit of rough.'

'What chap?'

'The one who runs the show. The owner.'

'Then it's a load of bollocks,' said Agatha, saying to herself, oh, Charles, how could you?

'Give my apologies,' said Agatha stiffly. 'No! Get off.'

Agatha drove home where she buried her face in her cats' fur and cried and cried. It was no use indulging in silly dreams of retirement and two pairs of slippers on the hearth. She had thought she meant more to Charles than a few one-night stands.

At last she dried her eyes and told the cats, 'I'm back to work full-time tomorrow.'

When Mrs Bloxby's guests moved to the drawing room for coffee, Charles approached Arthur. 'Why did Agatha leave?'

'It's not my fault,' said Arthur, turning red. 'She had this false eyelash that had come unstuck and she had tried to stick it back on with Super Glue. I told her nail varnish remover would do the trick and it did and she was flirting a lot so I grabbed her and she went all Lady Muck on me. But that chap at Barfield House, he told me she was the easiest lay in the Cotswolds and panting for it. I mean, he was the owner of the place.'

'I am the owner,' said Charles. 'Describe this man.'

Arthur said, 'Tall, grizzled hair, slight accent and–'

'Enough,' said Charles. 'Mrs Bloxby, lovely evening but I must rush. People to see. Heads to punch.'

Charles let himself into Agatha's cottage at six in the morning. His knuckles were sore under their bandages. He wished he hadn't punched Gustav so hard because Gustav wouldn't fight and simply sat there hunched up, saying Agatha was not suitable to be Charles's wife. Charles told him to pack his bags and leave. He was fired. But when Gustav left to collect his belongings, Charles thought wearily of all the work that Gustav did and what a success they were making of the haunted house and went and rehired him.

Agatha was lying asleep on her back, snoring, her mouth open and her face blotched with tears. Charles shook her by the shoulder and switched on the bedside lamp.

She looked at him blearily and then let out a squawk of rage. Charles imprisoned her hands and told her to listen and explained about Gustav. 'I'll kill him,' said Agatha. 'Oh, your hands are hurt. Did you fight him?'

Charles decided it was time to lie. He said in a light voice, 'I fought for your honour. You should have guessed it was Gustav. Why didn't you ask me? Do you think so little of yourself that you should believe one of your friends would trash you in that way? Look! Get up and get dressed and I'll take you for the full English breakfast.'

Agatha felt comforted after an enormous breakfast and three cups of coffee. 'I should really have taken Sir Edward with me to play Poirot but it was too dangerous. Poor old soul. Life must be dreary stuck in Cuckleton on his own.'

Sir Edward was indeed sunk in a deep depression. The day was cold and gloomy, the garden white with frost. Why had he ever decided to move to this dump? He heard a plop as the morning's mail came through the door. He wearily rose to get it. 'Bills, bills, bills,' he muttered, tearing open one after the other until he got to one in an embossed envelope. He opened it and let out a yelp. He had been appointed a peerage. He would be Lord something or other. Need to think of a title. Coat of arms. Robes. Oh, how absolutely bloody marvellous.

'It's absolutely bloody marvellous,' complained the other man called Edward Chumble to his wife. 'When I think of all the money I've given to the government for a peerage and I bet the bastards take the money and give me zilch!'

'Take me back home and I'll get my car. I'm going into the office,' said Agatha.
    'I thought you were retiring!'
    'I thought so, too,' said Agatha as they stood together in the car park. She took out a packet of cigarettes and a lighter and lit one up. 'I haven't given up the cancer sticks yet. You know, Charles, I should always remember what I was told all those years ago when my marriage to Jimmy

didn't work out.'

'What's that?'

'Careers last. Men don't.'

'You've always got me, Agatha.'

'As what?' A little gleam of hope flickered across Agatha's bearlike eyes.

Charles hesitated and then said brightly, 'As a friend.'

Simon hid in the shrubbery at the end of Lilac Lane and watched Charles drive off. He had come in the hope of confessing to Agatha that he had lied about Molly. He had made a pass at her and she had laughed, patted his head and told him to run along. He had actually gone to a brothel a friend had told him about and paid for a blowjob and left feeling dirty. But Agatha had looked so grim. Maybe another day.

Agatha let herself into her cottage. It was midday. She and Charles had spent the whole morning talking about the case. She went into the sitting room and stared at the drinks trolley as her cats weaved around her ankles.

'Well,' said Agatha, 'a woman needs a man like a fish ... needs a good, stiff gin and tonic!'

Other titles published by Ulverscroft:

DEATH OF A PERFECT WIFE

M. C. Beaton

Hamish Macbeth is savouring the delights of a Highland summer, but as fast as the rain rolls in from the loch, things start to unravel. The trouble begins when his beloved Priscilla Halburton-Smythe returns to Lochdubh with a new fiancé. His miseries multiply when clouds of midges descend on the town. And then a paragon of housewife perfection named Trixie Thomas moves into Lochdubh with her browbeaten husband in tow. The newcomer quickly convinces the local ladies to embrace low-cholesterol meals, ban alcohol and begin bird-watching. Soon the town's menfolk are up in arms and Macbeth must solve Lochdubh's newest crime — the mysterious poisoning of the perfect wife.

HOMECOMING

M. C. Beaton

Lizzie is the sixth and youngest daughter of the late Sir Beverley, the patriarch who gambled away their beloved estate, Mannerling. Each of Lizzie's sisters had been entrusted by their ambitious mother to lure the various owners of their former home. Instead, each one married for love. Now it's Lizzie's turn to save Mannerling. Yet the new owner, the Duke of Severnshire, is far too arrogant for Lizzie's heart. And while the duke has no intentions toward Lizzie, her curt dismissal is perplexing — for no woman has ever refused him! Soon thoughts turn away from a suitable marriage — to the wonders of falling in love!

DEATH OF A GHOST

M. C. Beaton

When Police Sergeant Hamish Macbeth hears reports of a haunted castle near Drim, he assumes the eerie noises and lights reported by the villagers are just local teenagers going there to smoke pot. Still, Hamish and his policeman, Charlie 'Clumsy' Carson, spend the night at the castle to find out. The keening wind explains the ghostly noises, but when Charlie falls through the floor, Hamish finds the body of a dead man propped up in a corner of the cellar. Charlie is airlifted to hospital and Chief Detective Inspector Blair investigates, but the body is missing. Hamish must find the body and its killer before the 'ghost' can strike again.